First French
PART ONE
AT HOME

Kathy Gemmell and Jenny Tyler
Illustrated by Sue Stitt
Designed by Diane Thistlethwaite

Consultants: Sarah-Lou Reekie and Kate Griffin

CONTENTS
(Part one)

6985

First published in 1993 by Usborne Publishing Ltd.
Usborne House, 83-85 Saffron Hill
London EC1N 8RT, England.
Copyright © 1993 Usborne Publishing Ltd.
First published in America August 1993.
Printed in Portugal.
Universal Edition.

Speaking French

This book is about the Noisette family. They are going to help you learn to speak French.

Word lists

You will find a word list on every double page to tell you what the French words mean.

Bonjour
bonjoor

The little letters are to help you say the French words. Read them as if they were English words.

Je...
je

Bonne nuit
bon nwee

Non
naw

Oui
we

Salut
salew

Word list

bonjour bonjoor	hello
salut salew	hi
non naw	no
oui we	yes
je je	I
bonne nuit bon nwee	good night
à toi ah twa	your turn

The best way to find out how to say French words is to listen to a French person speaking. Some sounds are a bit different from English. Here are some clues to help you.

When you see a "j" in French, say it like the middle sound in "treasure". Try saying *je*, which means "I".

When you see an "n" in French, be careful. Single "n"s are usually not pronounced. Only double "n"s or "n"s which come before a,e,i,o or u are pronounced.

To say the "u" in *salut*, round your lips to say "oo" then say "ee" instead.

Say the French "r" by making a rolling sound in the back of your mouth, a bit like gargling.

Try saying out loud what each person on this page is saying.

See if you can find Delphine the mouse on each double page.

Games with word lists

You can play games with the word lists if you like. Here are some ideas.

1. Cover all the French words and see if you can say the French for each English word. Score a point for each one you can remember.

2. Time yourself and see if you can say the whole list more quickly next time.

3. Race a friend. The first one to say the French for each word scores a point. The winner is the one to score the most points.

4. Play all these games the other way around, saying the English for each French word.

À toi
Look for the *à toi* boxes in this book. There is something for you to do in each of them. *À toi* means "your turn".

Look out for the joke bubbles on some of the pages.

The Noisettes

Here the Noisette family are introducing themselves. *Je m'appelle* [je mapell] means "I am called" or "my name is".

Loulou' has chased Delphine through the Noisette's garden. See if you can follow her route from Oncle Paul to where she is now. Which members of the family did she pass on the way?

Word list

je m'appelle	I am called
je mapell	
Monsieur	Mr.
miss yer	
Madame	Mrs.
ma dam	
la grand-mère	grandma
la gronmair	
l'oncle	uncle
lonkl	
la tante	aunt
la tont	
au revoir	goodbye
orvwar	

Names

Noisette	**Mirabelle**
nwa zet	meer a bel
Roger	**Paul**
rojay	pol
Sophie	**Hercule**
sofee	air kewl
Henri	**Loulou**
onree	looloo
Francine	**Delphine**
fronseen	delfeen
Jean	**Legs**
jon	legs
Robert	**Suzanne**
robair	sewz an

Je m'appelle Sophie.

Je m'appelle Roger.

Je m'appelle Hercule.

Je m'appelle Jean.

Je m'appelle Grand-mère Noisette.

Je m'appelle Francine.

Je m'appelle Henri.

Hello

Bonjour [bonjoor] means "hello". Sophie is so sleepy, she has mixed up everyone's names. Say *bonjour* for her, adding the correct name each time.

Bonjour Henri

Bonjour Grand-mère

4

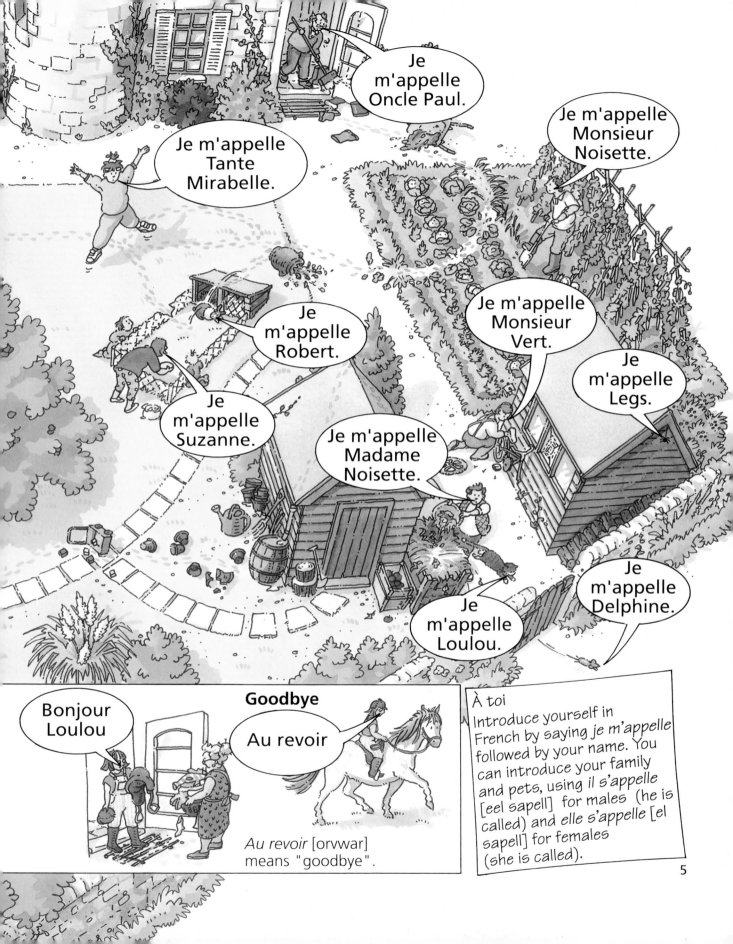

Au revoir [orvwar] means "goodbye".

À toi
Introduce yourself in French by saying je m'appelle followed by your name. You can introduce your family and pets, using il s'appelle [eel sapell] for males (he is called) and elle s'appelle [el sapell] for females (she is called).

5

At home

Here is the inside of the Noisette family house. Can you find a way around the house, passing all those who are waiting to tell you the names of the rooms on the way? You must not pass anyone more than once.

Start at the door nearest Madame Noisette and go out by the kitchen door. (Remember that doors are not the only way to get from room to room.)

Chez nous [shay noo] means "our home". "My home" is *chez moi* [shay mwa]. Anyone else's home is *chez* then the name of the person, so "Sophie's home" would be *chez Sophie* [shay sofee].

Word list	
voici vwasee	here is
la chambre la shombr	bedroom
la salle de bain la sal dba	bathroom
le grenier le grin ee ay	attic
la cave la kaav	cellar
la cuisine la kweezeen	kitchen
le salon le salaw	lounge
la salle à manger la sala monjay	dining room
la maison la mayzaw	house
le jardin le jarda	garden
maman ma maw	mum
chez nous shay noo	our home

Voici la chambre.

Voici le salon.

Voici le jardin.

Voici Maman.

Voici la maison.

Draw a map

Sophie and Henri have drawn a map of the area near their house and have written all the names in French.

Draw a map of your own area or somewhere you think you would like to live and label it in French.

l'église

le pont

la rivière

la ferme

8

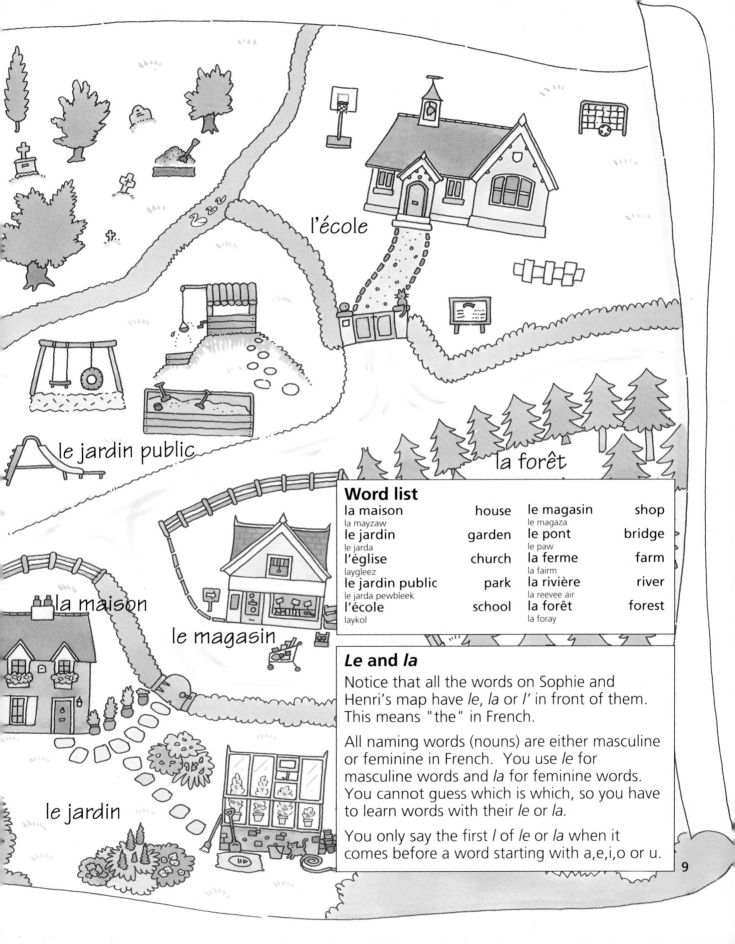

l'école

le jardin public

la forêt

la maison

le magasin

le jardin

Word list

la maison	house	**le magasin**	shop
la mayzaw		le magaza	
le jardin	garden	**le pont**	bridge
le jarda		le paw	
l'église	church	**la ferme**	farm
laygleez		la fairm	
le jardin public	park	**la rivière**	river
le jarda pewbleek		la reevee air	
l'école	school	**la forêt**	forest
laykol		la foray	

Le and *la*

Notice that all the words on Sophie and Henri's map have *le*, *la* or *l'* in front of them. This means "the" in French.

All naming words (nouns) are either masculine or feminine in French. You use *le* for masculine words and *la* for feminine words. You cannot guess which is which, so you have to learn words with their *le* or *la*.

You only say the first *l* of *le* or *la* when it comes before a word starting with a,e,i,o or u.

9

Counting in French

Sophie and Henri stayed up late to finish their map and now can't sleep. In fact, everybody is counting things to help them get to sleep.

Count out loud in French for each person. Who do you think fell asleep first? Use the number list to help you.

Number list

un a	one
deux deuh	two
trois trwa	three
quatre katr	four
cinq sank	five
six seess	six
sept set	seven
huit weet	eight
neuf neuf	nine
dix deess	ten

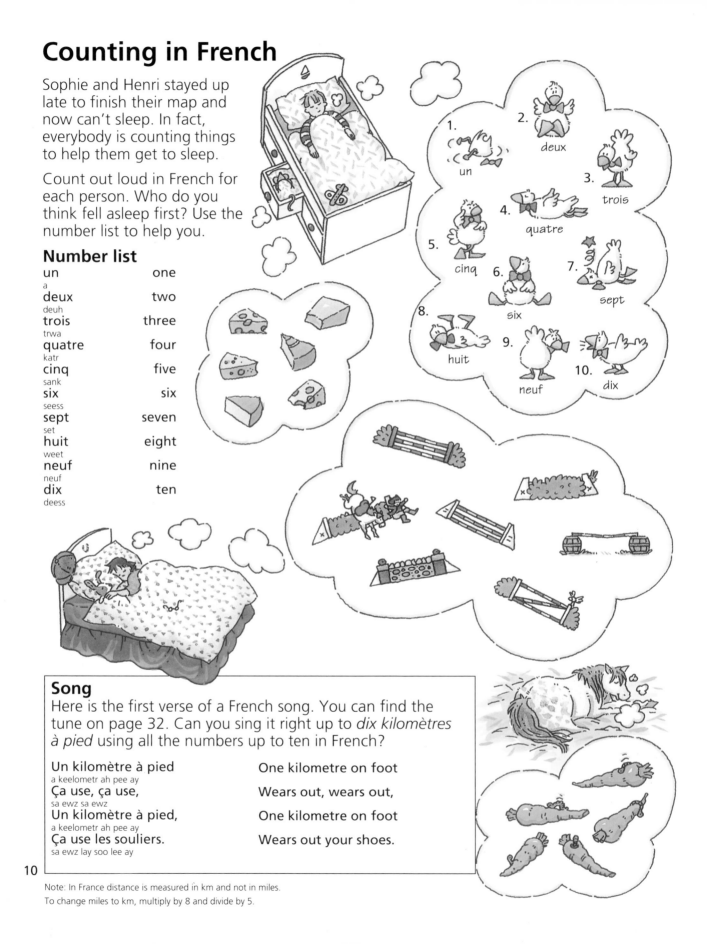

1. un
2. deux
3. trois
4. quatre
5. cinq
6. six
7. sept
8. huit
9. neuf
10. dix

Song

Here is the first verse of a French song. You can find the tune on page 32. Can you sing it right up to *dix kilomètres à pied* using all the numbers up to ten in French?

Un kilomètre à pied a keelometr ah pee ay	One kilometre on foot
Ça use, ça use, sa ewz sa ewz	Wears out, wears out,
Un kilomètre à pied, a keelometr ah pee ay	One kilometre on foot
Ça use les souliers. sa ewz lay soo lee ay	Wears out your shoes.

10

Note: In France distance is measured in km and not in miles.
To change miles to km, multiply by 8 and divide by 5.

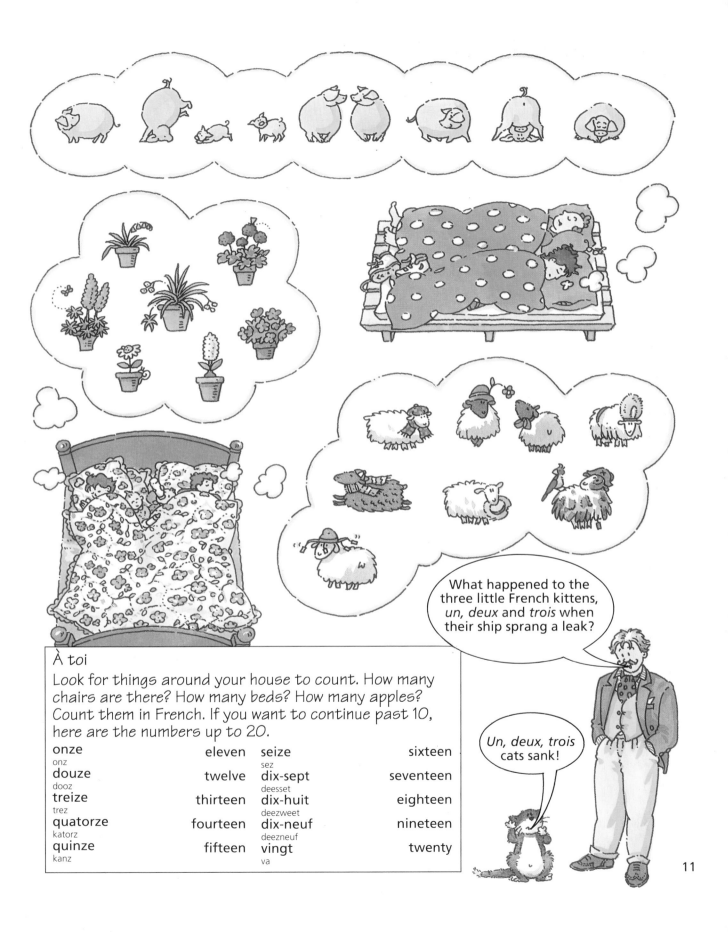

What happened to the three little French kittens, *un, deux* and *trois* when their ship sprang a leak?

Un, deux, trois cats sank!

À toi

Look for things around your house to count. How many chairs are there? How many beds? How many apples? Count them in French. If you want to continue past 10, here are the numbers up to 20.

onze onz	eleven	**seize** sez	sixteen
douze dooz	twelve	**dix-sept** deesset	seventeen
treize trez	thirteen	**dix-huit** deezweet	eighteen
quatorze katorz	fourteen	**dix-neuf** deezneuf	nineteen
quinze kanz	fifteen	**vingt** va	twenty

Jigsaw puzzles

The next morning everybody is tired and a little bit grumpy. Roger has brought down some jigsaw puzzles to try and cheer up the family. However, the pieces are all mixed up and Henri is the only one who can see what his puzzle is, *une pomme* (an apple).

Can you say in French what all the other puzzles should be? Use the picture list to help you. Only one of the missing pieces cannot be found anywhere. Who will not be able to finish their jigsaw?

Un and *une*

In French there are two ways to say "one", *un* or *une*. Both also mean "a" or "an". All *le* words are *un* words and all *la* words are *une* words.

Une pomme

Picture list

une prune ẽwn prewn **a plum**	**un ananas** an ananass **a pineapple**	**une banane** ewn banan **a banane**	**une pêche** ewn pesh **a peach**	
une poire ewn pwar **a pear**	**une orange** ewn oronj **an orange**	**une pomme** ewn pom **an apple**		

À toi
See if you can remember the words for all these fruits and say what's in your fruit bowl at home.

12

Answer these questions out loud in French.

Can you see what Delphine is eating? What would Hercule like to eat?

Song

Here is a song about the fruit and vegetables that Delphine likes and dislikes. Can you guess what any of them are? You can see what all the words mean on page 32.

Au clair de la lu - ne, ma sou - ris Del - phine
oh clair de la lew nuh ma soo ree del feen

Aime beau - coup les pru - nes et les au - ber - gines.
em bo koo lay prew nuh ay laze oh bair jeen

Elle n'aime pas les oign - ons, ni les pet - its pois,
el nem pa laze on yaw nee lay pt ee pwa

Et pour tous les cham - pign - ons, elle les donne au roi.
ay poor too lay shom peen yaw el lay don oh rwa

13

Joke: What's blue and square? An orange in disguise

What is it?

Grand-mère has ordered lots of new things for her room. They have just been delivered. *Qu'est-ce que c'est?* [kess ke sai] means "what is it?"

Can you help the rest of the family say in French what is in each parcel? Say *c'est* [sai] which means "it is" and then the object. Use the picture list to help you with the names.

Remember that *un* and *une* both mean "a" as well as "one" in French.

Picture list

une table
ewn tabl
a table

une chaise
ewn shez
a chair

un lit
a lee
a bed

une télévision
ewn tay lay veezee aw
a television

un vase
a vaz
a vase

un réveil
a rave eye
an alarm clock

une lampe
ewn lomp
a lamp

une tasse
ewn tass
a cup

une assiette
ewn ass ee ett
a plate

À toi
Can you find all the things on the picture list in your own house? If you can, point to each one and say what it is in French, using *c'est* [sai] and then the name of the object.

15

Joke: What's this? It's this upside-down.

A day in the life of the Noisettes

This is a picture strip of a typical weekend day in the Noisette household - after a good night's sleep this time - but the pictures are all in the wrong order. Can you decide which order they should be in?

Use the word list to help you to say out loud what everyone is saying.

Word list

le petit déjeuner le ptee day je nay	breakfast
le déjeuner le day je nay	lunch
le dîner le deenay	dinner
du matin dew mata	in the morning
de l'après-midi de laprai meedee	in the afternoon
bonjour bonjoor	hello, good morning
bonsoir bonswar	good evening
bonne nuit bon nwee	good night
c'est sai	it is
dors bien dor beea	sleep well
il est 3 heures eel ai trwazer	it is three o'clock
il est 8 heures eel ai weeter	it is eight o'clock

Here is a little rhyme about Robert. Can you spot him in two of the pictures?

Le petit lapin
le ptee lapa
Se lève le matin
se lev le mata
Puis venu le soir
pwee vin ew le swar
Il dit "au revoir".
eel dee orvwar

You can check what all the words mean on page 32.

Bon appétit [bon a ptee] is what you say before eating in France. It means "enjoy your meal".

À table [ah tabl] is how you tell people in French to come to the table.

Afternoon activity

This afternoon the Noisettes are all busy doing things in and around the house. Can you find someone doing each of the things on the word list somewhere in the big picture?

As you find each one, read out loud what that person is saying in French.

Word list

je mange	I am eating
je monj	
je lis	I am reading
je lee	
je cours	I am running
je koor	
je marche	I am walking
je marsh	
je chante	I am singing
je shont	
je bois	I am drinking
je bwa	
je parle	I am speaking
je parl	
je dors	I am sleeping
je dor	
je sors	I am going out
je sor	
je saute	I am jumping
je sote	
je travaille	I am working
je trav eye	
je tombe	I am falling
je tom b	
je nage	I am swimming
je naj	

À toi

Qu'est-ce que tu fais? [kess ke tew fai]. *What are you doing at the moment? You're probably reading, so you say je lis [je lee]. See if you can do all the other things in the picture and remember how to say them in French.*

18

Joke: What has eight legs and spins? A spider in a washing machine.

Happy birthday

The next day is Grand-mère's birthday and the family is having a party for her. There are lots of different kinds of food because everyone likes different things.

To say you like something in French you say *j'aime* [jem] and then the thing you like. To say you don't like something you say *je n'aime pas* [je nem pa] and then the thing you don't like.

"Happy birthday" in French is *bon anniversaire* [bon anee vairsair].

Word list

j'aime jem	I like
je n'aime pas je nem pa	I don't like
moi mwa	me
les fruits lay frwee	fruit
le fromage le fromaj	cheese
le pain le pa	bread
les légumes lay laygewm	vegetables
la confiture la konfeetewr	jam
le chocolat le shokola	chocolate
la salade la sa lad	salad
le jambon le jombaw	ham
la soupe la soop	soup
les frites lay freet	french fries
les gâteaux lay ga toe	cakes
les saucisses lay soseess	sausages

J'aime le jambon.

Bon anniversaire.

J'aime le pain.

J'aime la confiture.

J'aime le chocolat.

Can you see which people do not like the food in front of them? Say out loud in French what they are thinking.

What do you think Sophie is saying? How would Hercule say what he likes in French?

À toi

Qu'est-ce que tu aimes manger? [kess ke tew em monjay] means "what do you like to eat?" Answer this question out loud in French. Remember, if you like something say *j'aime* [jem]. If you *don't* like something say *je n'aime pas* [je nem pa].

Le and *la* both change to *les* when you are talking about more than one thing.

21

Sophie goes shopping

Today is a school holiday and Sophie has gone to do the shopping.

Can you see from the picture what Sophie is asking for? *Je voudrais* [je voodray] means "I would like" and *et* [ay] means "and".

Now try to ask for all the items on Sophie's shopping list in French. Remember to say "please", *s'il vous plaît* [seel voo plai] and "thank you", *merci* [mairsee].

The money used in France is *francs* and *centimes*. There are 100 *centimes* to 1 *franc*.

Je voudrais un journal et une glace, s'il vous plaît.

Liste
4 pommes
9 bananes
8 petits pains
5 oignons
6 poissons
2 gâteaux

Can you see from the picture how to say "How much is it?" in French? Say it out loud.

What do you think Jean will ask for? Say it for him.

Number reminder

un	one	six	six
a		seess	
deux	two	sept	seven
deuh		set	
trois	three	huit	eight
trwa		weet	
quatre	four	neuf	nine
katr		neuf	
cinq	five	dix	ten
sank		deess	

À toi
Combien [kombeea] means "how much" and "how many" in French. Can you answer the following questions by looking at the picture? Use the number reminder to help you count up in French how many there are.

Combien de fleurs?
Combien de chapeaux?
Combien de chats?

22

Word list

je voudrais *je voodray*	I would like
un chat *a sha*	a cat
une pomme *ewn pom*	an apple
une banane *ewn banan*	a banana
un petit pain *a ptee pa*	a roll
un oignon *an onyaw*	an onion
un poisson *a pwassaw*	a fish
un journal *a joornal*	a newspaper
une fleur *ewn flur*	a flower
un gâteau *a gatoe*	a cake
une glace *ewn glas*	an ice cream cone
c'est combien? *sai kombeea*	how much is it?
c'est ... francs *sai ... fraw*	it is ... francs
s'il vous plaît *seel voo plai*	please
merci *mairsee*	thank you
un chapeau *a shapo*	a hat

Joke: What do you call a monkey who likes cakes? A meringue-utan.

Market day

Later on, the whole family goes down to the market. Everybody in the village seems to be there. It is so crowded that the Noisettes have split up and are all doing things in different parts of the market.

Jean asks where Robert is and the butcher points to him. *Où est* [oo ai] means "where is" and *Robert est là* [robair ai la] means "Robert is there".

Can you spot all of the Noisettes in the crowd? Point to each one and say that person's name followed by *est là* [ai la].

Où est Loulou?

Où est Delphine?

Où est Hercule?

Où est Robert?

Robert est là.

Merci, monsieur

Où
oo
vas-tu?
va tew

Je déménage.
je day may naj

24

Joke: Where are you going? I'm moving (house).

25

Dominoes to make

For something to do at home, Sophie and Henri have invented a game of dominoes which uses French colours. Here's how to make one like theirs and play it.

1. Cut your cardboard into 28 rectangles about 8cm long and 4cm wide (3in by 1½in). You can make the rectangles bigger if you have more cardboard.

4cm

8cm

You will need:
white cardboard (at least 32cm by 28 cm, 13in by 11in), felt tips, scissors and a black pen.

2. Copy the colours and words from the small dominoes shown here onto your rectangles. Use the colour guide to help you.

3. The idea of the game is to fit all the dominoes into a pattern, matching up the colours as shown below. If you are playing by yourself, the double-red starts.

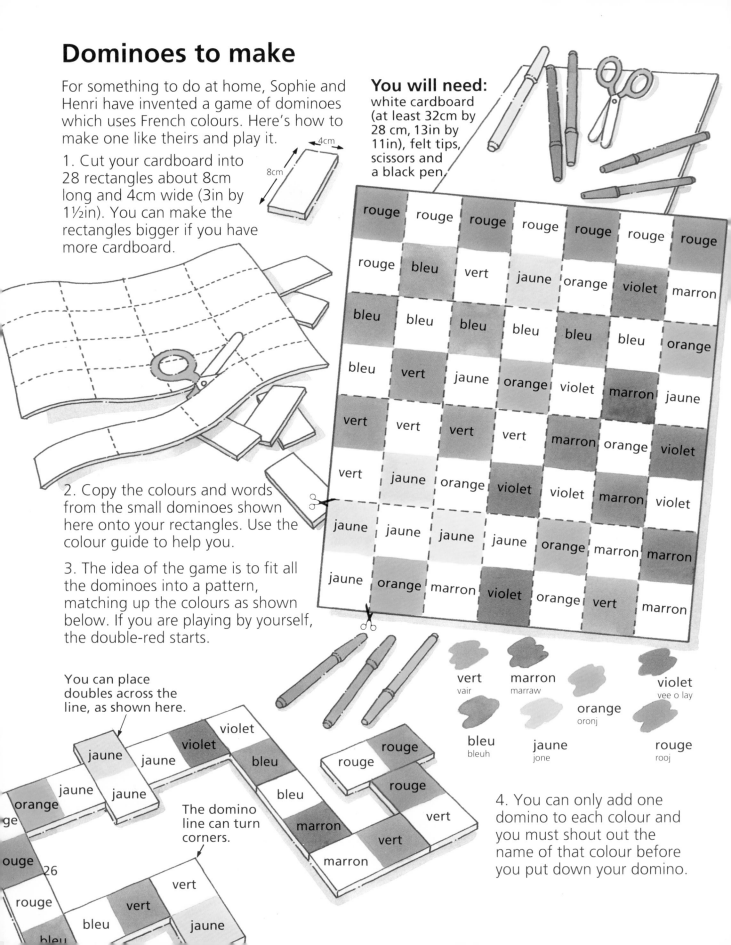

rouge	rouge	rouge	rouge	rouge	rouge	rouge
rouge	bleu	vert	jaune	orange	violet	marron
bleu	bleu	bleu	bleu	bleu	bleu	orange
bleu	vert	jaune	orange	violet	marron	jaune
vert	vert	vert	vert	marron	orange	violet
vert	jaune	orange	violet	violet	marron	violet
jaune	jaune	jaune	jaune	orange	marron	marron
jaune	orange	marron	violet	orange	vert	marron

You can place doubles across the line, as shown here.

The domino line can turn corners.

vert
vair

marron
marraw

violet
vee o lay

orange
oronj

bleu
bleuh

jaune
jone

rouge
rooj

4. You can only add one domino to each colour and you must shout out the name of that colour before you put down your domino.

26

5. If you are playing with a friend, first spread the dominoes out, face-down, on the table or floor. Take seven dominoes each and put them face-up in front of you. These form your "hand".

6. The idea of this game is to get rid of all the dominoes in your hand and the first person to do so is the winner.

7. The first person to put down a double and shout out what colour it is (in French) starts. Take turns to match your dominoes with the colours or colour words at either end of the domino line, each time shouting out the colour in French before putting down your domino.

8. If you can't go, you must pick up a spare domino if there is one left, or miss a turn if there is not.

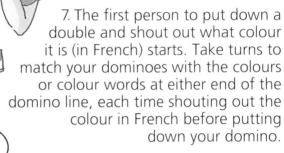

À toi

J'ai gagné.

Word list

à toi	your turn
ah twa	
j'ai gagné	I 've won
jay ganyay	

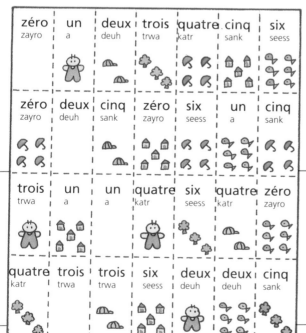

zéro	un	deux	trois	quatre	cinq	six
zayro	a	deuh	trwa	katr	sank	seess

zéro	deux	cinq	zéro	six	un	cinq
zayro	deuh	sank	zayro	seess	a	sank

trois	un	un	quatre	six	quatre	zéro
trwa	a	a	katr	seess	katr	zayro

quatre	trois	trois	six	deux	deux	cinq
katr	trwa	trwa	seess	deuh	deuh	sank

Number dominoes

You could also make French number dominoes. Copy these dominoes onto pieces of cardboard (the same as the ones used for Colour dominoes) and play in the same way, this time matching up the number of objects with the number in French. The double-six fish starts.

27

Memory game

Here is a game which you can play again and again. The idea is to get to the finish as quickly as possible.

You will need:
a dice
a clock or watch

How to play

Look at the time when you start. Throw the dice and count with your finger the number of squares shown on the dice. Say the answer to the question on that square out loud then shake again.

If you land on a square with no question on it, shake again and move on.

All the answers can be found in this part of the book, so if you can't remember or are not sure, look back through the book until you find the correct answer.

Look at the time again when you finish. Can you do it more quickly next time?

How would you say the word for church in French, *l'église?*

1. lie gliss
2. lay gleez
3. liggles

Tell Henri how to ask for an ice cream cone in French.

Combien de fleurs?

Say "yes" in French.

Say "hi" in French.

What would Henri say if you asked, *Qu'est-ce que tu fais?*

Qu'est-ce que c'est?

How do you introduce yourself in French?

1. bleu
2. violet
3. jaune

Say "hello" in French.

Which of these describes Francine's balloon?

What is Sophie saying to Monsieur Vert?

Say "good night" in French.

Which of these is Sophie saying?

Say "I am eating" in French.

1. J'aime le fromage
2. J'aime le jambon
3. J'aime les bonbons

How will Henri tell his friend what Delphine's name is?

Départ
daypar
(start)

What comes after dix-huit?

Qu'est-ce que c'est?

Qu'est-ce que c'est?

How do you say "the garden" in French?

Which of these numbers is in the wrong place?

un deux cinq trois quatre

How would you ask for an apple in French?

How would you say "a peach" in French?

1. ewn peck
2. un pish
3. ewn pesh

Say the missing word, c'est une...

How do you say "my home" in French?

Qu'est-ce que c'est?

Say "thank you" in French.

20

How do you say "twenty" in French?

Which room do you think Hercule is in? Say it in French.

Qu'est-ce que c'est?

What happened to the three little French kittens, un, deux and trois, when their ship sprang a leak?

What comes after sept?

15

How do you say "fifteen" in French?

How will Sophie say what she is doing in French?

Qu'est-ce que c'est?

What do you say in France before starting a meal?

Qu'est-ce que c'est?

Say "good-bye" in French.

How do you say "how much is it?" in French?

Combien de pommes?

How would you say voici?

What would Jean say if you asked, Qu'est-ce que tu fais, Jean?

1. voy zee
2. vwasee
3. vwokay

Fin
fa
(end)

29

Word list (part one)

Here is a list, in alphabetical order, of all the French words and phrases used in this part of the book. Use the list either to check quickly what a word means, or to test yourself. The [m] or [f] after *l'* words tell you whether the word is a *le* word (masculine) or a *la* word (feminine).

à pied	ah pee ay	on foot
à table	ah tabl	dinner's ready!
à toi	ah twa	your turn
ananas (l') [m]	ananass	pineapple
araignée (l') [f]	a renyay	spider
assiette (l') [f]	ass ee ett	plate
aubergine (l') [f]	oh bair jeen	aubergine, eggplant
au clair de	oh clair de	by the light of
la lune	la lewn	the moon
au revoir	orvwar	goodbye
banane (la)	banan	banana
beaucoup	bokoo	a lot
bleu	bleuh	blue
bon anniversaire	bon anee vairsair	happy birthday
bon appétit	bon a ptee	enjoy your meal
bonjour	bonjoor	hello
bonne nuit	bon nwee	good night
bonsoir	bonswar	good evening
ça use	sa ewz	it wears out
carré	karry	square
cave (la)	kaav	cellar
c'est	sai	it is
c'est combien?	sai kombeea	how much is it?
chaise (la)	shez	chair
chambre (la)	shombr	bedroom
champignon (le)	shompeenyaw	mushroom
chapeau (le)	shapo	hat
chat (le)	sha	cat
chez moi	shay mwa	my home
chocolat (le)	shokola	chocolate
cinq	sank	five
combien	kombeea	how many, how much
confiture (la)	konfeetewr	jam
cuisine (la)	kweezeen	kitchen
dans	daw	in
de l'après-midi	de laprai meedee	in the afternoon
déguisée	day geezay	in disguise
déjeuner (le)	day je nay	lunch
départ	daypar	start
deux	deuh	two
dîner (le)	deenay	dinner
dix	deess	ten

dix-huit	deezweet	eighteen
dix-neuf	deezneuf	nineteen
dix-sept	deesset	seventeen
dors bien	dor beea	sleep well
douze	dooz	twelve
du matin	dew mata	in the morning
école (l') [f]	aykol	school
église (l') [f]	aygleez	church
elle	el	she, it
elle est	el ai	she is, it is
elle est là	el ai la	she/it is there
elle s'appelle	el sapell	she is called
et	ay	and
ferme (la)	fairm	farm
fin	fa	end
fleur (la)	flur	flower
forêt (la)	foray	forest
frites (les) [f]	freet	french fries
fromage (le)	fromaj	cheese
fruit (le)	frwee	fruit
gâteau (le)	ga toe	cake
glace (la)	glas	ice cream cone
grand-mère (la)	gronmair	grandmother
grenier (le)	grin ee ay	attic
huit	weet	eight
il	eel	he, it
il dit	eel dee	he says
il est	eel ai	he is, it is
il est là	eel ai la	he/it is there
il s'appelle	eel sapell	he is called
il se lève	eel se lev	he gets up
j'ai gagné	jay ganyay	I've won
j'aime	jem	I like
jambon (le)	jombaw	ham
jardin (le)	jarda	garden
jardin public (le)	jarda pewbleek	park
jaune	jone	yellow
je	je	I
je bois	je bwa	I am drinking
je chante	je shont	I am singing
je cours	je koor	I am running
je déménage	je day may naj	I am moving (house)
je dors	je dor	I am sleeping
je lis	je lee	I am reading
je mange	je monj	I am eating
je m'appelle	je mapell	I am called
je marche	je marsh	I am walking

French	Pronunciation	English
je nage	je naj	I am swimming
je n'aime pas	je nem pa	I don't like
je parle	je parl	I am speaking
je saute	je sote	I am jumping
je sors	je sor	I am going out
je tombe	je tom b	I am falling
je travaille	je trav eye	I am working
je voudrais	je voodray	I would like
journal (le)	joornal	newspaper
kilomètre (le)	keelometr	kilometre
là	la	there
lampe (la)	lomp	lamp
lapin (le)	lapa	rabbit
le, la, les	le, la, lay	the
légume (le)	laygewm	vegetable
lit (le)	lee	bed
machine	masheen	washing
à laver (la)	a lavay	machine
Madame	ma dam	Mrs.
magasin (le)	magaza	shop
maison (la)	mayzaw	house
maman	ma maw	mum
marron	marraw	brown
merci	mairsee	thank you
moi	mwa	me
Monsieur	missyer	Mr.
neuf	neuf	nine
non	naw	no
nous	noo	we, us
oignon (l') [m]	onyaw	onion
oncle (l') [m]	onkl	uncle
onze	onz	eleven
orange (l') [f]	oronj	orange
où est...?	oo ai	where is...?
où vas-tu?	oo va tew	where are you going?
oui	wee	yes
pain (le)	pa	bread
papa	papa	dad
patte (la)	pat	leg (of an animal)
pêche (la)	peach	peach
petit	ptee	small
petit déjeuner (le)	ptee day je nay	breakfast
petit pain (le)	ptee pa	roll
petits pois (les)	ptee pwa	peas
poire (la)	pwar	pear
poisson (le)	pwassaw	fish
pomme (la)	pom	apple
pont (le)	paw	bridge
prune (la)	prewn	plum
puis	pwee	then
quatorze	katorz	fourteen
quatre	katr	four
qui	kee	who
quinze	kanz	fifteen
qu'est-ce que c'est?	kess ke sai	what is it?
qu'est-ce que tu aimes manger?	kess ke tew em monjay	what do you like to eat?
qu'est-ce que tu fais?	kess ke tew fai	what are you doing?
retourné	retoornay	upside-down
réveil (le)	rave eye	alarm clock
rivière (la)	reevee air	river
roi (le)	rwa	king
rouge	rooj	red
salade (la)	sa lad	salad
salle à manger (la)	sala monjay	dining room
salle de bain (la)	sal dba	bathroom
salon (le)	salaw	lounge
salut	salew	hi
saucisse (la)	soseess	sausage
seize	sez	sixteen
sept	set	seven
singe (le)	sanj	monkey
s'il vous plaît	seel voo plai	please
six	seess	six
soir (le)	swar	evening
souliers (les) [m]	soolee ay	shoes
soupe (la)	soop	soup
souris (la)	sooree	mouse
table (la)	tabl	table
tante (la)	tont	aunt
tasse (la)	tass	cup
télévision (la)	taylay veezee aw	television
tourne en rond	toorn aw raw	spins
treize	trez	thirteen
trois	trwa	three
tu	tew	you
un, une	a, ewn	a, one
vase (le)	vaz	vase
vert	vair	green
vingt	va	twenty
violet	vee o lay	purple
voici	vwasee	here is
zéro	zayro	zero

Answers (part one)

PAGE 4-5

Loulou passed *Oncle Paul, Monsieur Noisette, Robert, Tante Mirabelle, Jean, Roger, Sophie, Hercule, Francine, Henri, Grand-mère* and *Madame Noisette.*

Sophie should say *Bonjour Loulou, Bonjour Henri* and *Bonjour Grand-mère.*

PAGE 6-7

This is the way you must go:

PAGE 10-11

Hercule fell asleep first - he only counted to five before falling asleep.
Try to learn the numbers in the number list. Then see if you can sing up to *dix kilomètres à pied* without looking at the number words.

The tune for the song is:

PAGE 12-13

What everyone's jigsaws were:
    Monsieur Noisette-*une pêche* (a peach),
    Tante Mirabelle-*une poire* (a pear),
    Suzanne-*une banane* (a banana),
    Francine-*un ananas* (a pineapple),
    Jean-*une prune* (a plum),
    Sophie-*une orange* (an orange).

Monsieur Noisette will not be able to finish his jigsaw.

The answers to the questions are:
    Delphine - *une prune* (a plum),
    Hercule - *une pomme* (an apple).

Here is what the words in the song mean in English:
    By the light of the moon
    My mouse Delphine
    Loves plums
    And aubergines.
    She doesn't like onions
    Nor peas
    And as for all the mushrooms
    She gives them to the king.

PAGE 16-17

The right order for the pictures is: D F G H B E C A

Here is the rhyme in English:
    My little rabbit
    Gets up in the morning
    And when evening comes
    He says "goodbye".

PAGE 20-21

Henri is thinking *Je n'aime pas le fromage.*
Roger is thinking *Je n'aime pas la soupe.*
Oncle Paul is thinking *Je n'aime pas les saucisses.*
Sophie is saying *J'aime les frites.*
Hercule would say *J'aime les fruits.*

PAGE 22-23

Sophie is asking for a newspaper and an ice cream cone.

"How much is it?" is *c'est combien?*

Jean is going to say *Je voudrais une glace, s'il vous plaît.*

There are:
    9 fleurs
    5 chapeaux
    6 chats.

First French

PART 2: ON HOLIDAY

Kathy Gemmell and Jenny Tyler
Illustrated by Sue Stitt
Designed by Diane Thistlethwaite

Consultants: Sarah-Lou Reekie and Kate Griffin

CONTENTS

(part 2)

In this part of the book the Noisettes are at the beach for a week. They are going to help you to learn more French.

Remember that you will find a word list on every double page to tell you what the French words mean.

Bonjour
bonjoor

Salut
salew

Don't forget that the little letters are to help you say the French words.

Je m'appelle
je mapell
Roger.
ro jay

Il s'appelle
eel sapell
Roger.
rojay

Je parle
je parl
français.
fronsai

Bonsoir
bonswar

Word list

bonjour bonjoor	hello
salut salew	hi
je m'appelle je mapell	I am called
il s'appelle eel sapell	he is called
je parle français je parl fronsai	I speak French
le jeu le jeuh	the game
bonsoir bonswar	good evening

Try to listen to real French people speaking whenever you can. Here are more clues to help you say some of the French sounds.

The French "eu" sounds like the "e" in "the". *Je, le* and *de* end in the same sound. Say *le jeu* [le jeuh] which means "the game".

Both "i" and "y" sound like the "ee" in "see", but shorter. Try saying *il s'appelle* [eel sapell] which means "he is called".

Remember to roll French "r"s in the back of your mouth. Say *je parle français* [je parl fronsai] which means "I speak French".

Although single "n"s are hardly pronounced, you will sound French if you imagine you have a cold when you say words like *bonsoir* [bonswar], which means "good evening".

Can you say out loud what each person is saying?

Remember to look for Delphine the mouse on each double page.

Les jeux - games

Remember that you can play games with the word lists if you like. Trying to remember the French for each English word is a very good way to learn.

Did you notice that *les jeux* [lay jeuh], "games", is written differently from the word for "game" on the word list? Usually you add an "s" to words to make them plural (when there is more than one), but with some words you add an "x" instead.

Can you find other words in this part of the book which need an "x" on the end to make them plural? You can check that you have found them all on page 64.

À toi
Don't forget that *à toi* means "your turn". Remember to look for the *à toi* boxes in this part of the book.

Remember to look out for the joke bubbles on some of the pages.

Setting off

The Noisette family are getting ready to go away to the beach for a week. Unfortunately, everyone seems to have lost something.

Can you help by answering all of their questions? *Où est* [oo ai] means "where is". Use the word list to see what the other words mean.

Everything can be found somewhere in the picture. Point to each missing object and say "there it is" in French. This is *le voilà* [le vwala] if the object has *le* before it, or *la voilà* [la vwala] if the object has *la* before it.

Word list

où est oo ai	where is
le voilà le vwala	there he/it is
la voilà la vwala	there she/it is
la balle la bal	ball
le journal le joornal	newspaper
la canne à pêche la kan a pesh	fishing rod
le panier le panee ay	basket
le parapluie le para plewee	umbrella
la radio la radeeo	radio
la serviette la serv ee et	towel
la voiture la vwa chewr	car
la grand-mère gronmair	grandma
Monsieur miss yer	Mr.

Names

Noisette   Sophie   Francine
nwa zet   sofee   fronseen

Le and *la*

Remember that *le* and *la* both mean "the". In French, all naming words (nouns) are either masculine or feminine.

Masculine words have *le* before them and feminine words have *la* before them. You cannot guess which is which, so you have to learn words with their *le* or *la*.

Don't forget that *le* and *la* both change to *les* [lay] when there is more than one thing (plural).

37

Joke: What's yellow and black and wears a straw hat? A bee on holiday.

En route

The Noisettes quickly get lost. They've also lost some of their luggage on the way. Can you find it for them by following their route so far? Start at their house, which is *chez les Noisette* [shay lay nwa zet] in French.

Now they want to see all the places on the word list on their way to the beach. Which way should they go? They can only pass each place once.

Word list

Remember, *le* and *la* mean "the".

la chaumière la show me air	cottage
le camping le kompeeng	campsite
le château le sha toe	castle
le café le kafay	café
la gare la gar	station
le lac le lak	lake
la forêt la foray	forest
la ferme la fairm	farm
la maison bleue la mayzaw bleuh	blue house
le marché le marshay	market
la plage la plaj	beach

Can you find the windmill, the field, the church and the school on the map? Point to them and say their names out loud in French.

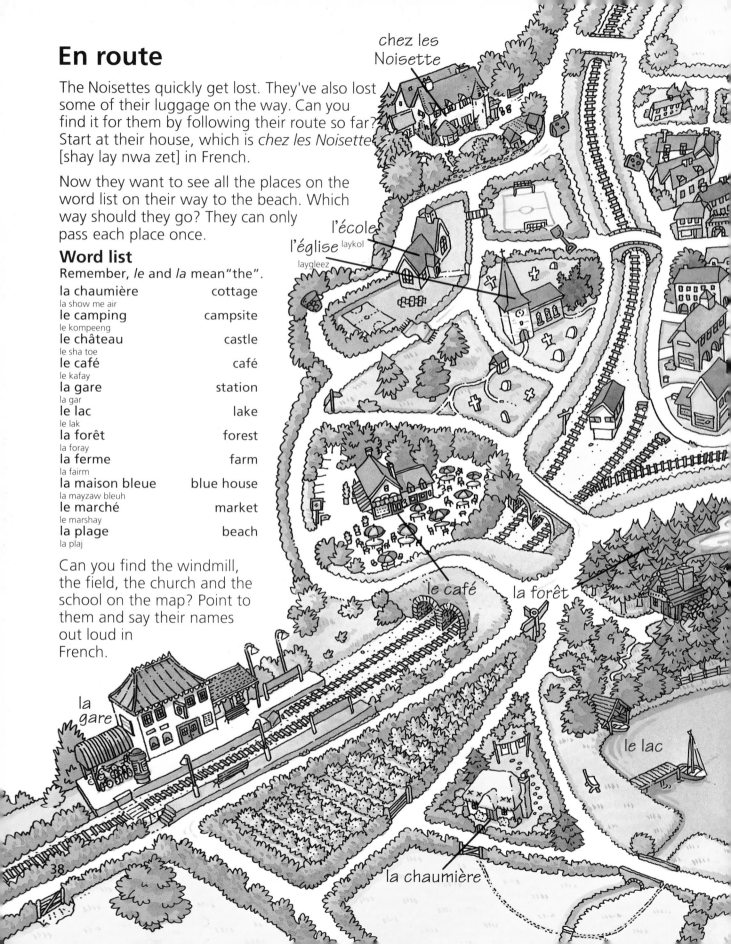

chez les Noisette

l'école laykol

l'église laygleez

le café

la forêt

la gare

le lac

la chaumière

38

le marché

la plage

le moulin
à vent
le moola a vaw

le château

la maison
bleue

la ferme
le champ
le shaw

À toi
Imagine you're going
away for a week. Draw a
map showing where you
are going and label all
the places you will pass
in French.

le camping

39

Counting game

Sophie, Henri, Francine and Jean set off to explore the countryside around the chalet where they are staying. In the forest they play a game to see who can spot the most wildlife. They write down how many of each thing they see.

Only one person has counted everything correctly. Can you see from their lists and the picture who it is?

Use the number key and word list to help you with the words.

Word list

une souris ewn sooree	a mouse	les renards lay rnar	foxes
les souris lay sooree	mice	les papillons lay pap ee yaw	butterflies
un chat, les chats a sha, lay sha	a cat, cats	les arbres laze arbr	trees
les lapins lay lapa	rabbits	les fleurs lay flur	flowers
les cerfs lay serr	deer	un nid, les nids a nee, lay nee	a nest, nests
les oiseaux laze wazo	birds	combien (de) kombeea	how many
les serpents lay sairpaw	snakes	il y a eel ya	there is/are

Number key

un a	one	six seess	six
deux deuh	two	sept set	seven
trois trwa	three	huit weet	eight
quatre katr	four	neuf neuf	nine
cinq sank	five	dix deess	ten

Names

Henri
onree

Jean
jon

How many?

In French, "How many... are there?" is *Il y a combien de...?* [eel ya kombeea de]. To answer, you say *Il y a* [eel ya] and then the number of things. So to answer *Il y a combien de chats?* [eel ya kombeea de sha] you would say *Il y a deux chats* [eel ya deuh sha]. Can you answer the following questions in French?

Il y a combien d'arbres?

Il y a combien de nids?

Il y a combien de fleurs?

Henri
sept oiseaux
huit lapins
une souris
six cerfs
quatre renards
deux chats
cinq papillons
trois serpents

Francine
huit oiseaux
sept lapins
deux souris
trois cerfs
cinq renards
un chat
dix papillons
deux serpents

Jean
huit oiseaux
huit lapins
une souris
trois cerfs
quatre renards
un chat
neuf papillons
deux serpents

Sophie
huit oiseaux
huit lapins
trois souris
quatre cerfs
quatre renards
un chat
sept papillons
deux serpents

40 *Joke: What's the difference between an African elephant and an Indian elephant? 10 000km. (In France, distance is measured in km, not miles. To change miles to km, multiply by 8 and divide by 5.)

On the beach

On the first day at the beach, the Noisette children join a beach club. To help everyone get to know each other, they have all made name and age badges to wear.

Quel âge as-tu? [kel aj a tew] means "How old are you?" Francine answers, *J'ai sept ans* [jay settaw], which means "I am seven".

Can you say in French what Jean, Henri and Sophie are saying? What would either of the twins say? Use the number list to help you.

Number list

un a	one	six seess	six
deux deuh	two	sept set	seven
trois trwa	three	huit weet	eight
quatre katr	four	neuf neuf	nine
cinq sank	five	dix deess	ten

Word list

quel âge as-tu? kel aj a tew	how old are you?
j'ai...ans jay aw	I'm...years old
comment tu t'appelles? kommaw tew tapell	what are you called?
je m'appelle je mapell	I am called, my name is

À toi

Make your own name and age badge in French. You will need: a piece of cardboard, a safety pin, sticky tape, a pen or pencil, scissors and a cup or mug.

1. Draw a circle on the piece of cardboard, using the bottom of a cup (or any round object of the size you want your badge to be) to draw a perfect circle. Then cut it out.

2. *Comment tu t'appelles?* [kommaw tew tapell]. Write on the circle what you are called and how old you are in French. *Je m'appelle* [je mapell] means "I am called". Look at the picture to see how to write how old you are.

Je m'appelle Henri.
J'ai huit ans.

3. Stick a pin to the back of the circle with sticky tape.(Remember to only stick down one side of the pin so that it can still open).

Treasure hunt

Claude [klode], the leader of the beach club, has organized a treasure hunt. He has hidden the treasure in one of the red boxes in the picture.

Using the word and picture lists to help you, can you follow the clues below to find out which of the red boxes holds the treasure?

As you say each clue out loud in French, point to any of the red boxes you can see in that place. The treasure box is the only one which is in all the places on the list of clues.

Les indices (Clues)
Dans le camping
Derrière la tente
Devant l'arbre
À côté de la barrière
Sur le mur
Sous le seau

Word list

le camping *le kompeeng*	campsite
la barrière *la ba ree air*	gate
l'arbre *larbr*	tree
la tente *la tont*	tent
le mur *le mewr*	wall
le seau *le so*	bucket

Picture list

derrière *derry air*

sur *sewr*

sous *soo*

devant *de vaw*

dans *daw*

à côté de *ah cotai de*

À toi

You could make up your own treasure hunt using French clues. Hide something and write down how to find it in French using Claude's clues and/or any of the phrases below.

Derrière le rideau
derry air le reedo

Sous la table
soo la tabl

Devant le canapé
devaw le kanapai

Sous le lit
soo le lee

Sur le rocher
sewr le roshay

Dans le panier à linge
daw le panee ay a lanj

Devant la glace
de vaw la glas

À côté de la plante
ah cotai de la plont

Derrière la corbeille à papier
derry air la korbaee a papeeay

Dans le placard
daw le plakar

À côté de la télévision
ah cotai de la taylay veezee aw

Guess who?

Claude's next activity for the beach club is the Guess who? game. Everyone must pretend to be someone or something else. Claude must guess what each child is pretending to be.

Can you see who is a mouse? Who is a king? *Je suis* [je swee] means "I am". Using the word list to help you, say out loud in French what each child is thinking.

Word list

je suis je swee	I am	**une fille** ewn feey	a girl
tu es tew ai	you are	**un garçon** a garssaw	a boy
oui wee	yes	**un homme** an om	a man
non naw	no	**un oiseau** a wazo	a bird
un chat a sha	a cat	**une reine** ewn ren	a queen
un cheval a shval	a horse	**un roi** a rwa	a king
un chien a sheea	a dog	**une souris** ewn sooree	a mouse
une femme ewn fam	a woman		

46

Claude has aready guessed what three people are. *Tu es* [tew ai] means "you are".

Can you say in French what he will say to all the others when he guesses what they are pretending to be?

À toi

What are you?
You could play a Guess who? game in French with friends.

How to play:

Choose someone to be the first guesser. All the other players act out what they would like to be.

The guesser shouts out in French when he guesses someone, using *tu es* [tew ai] then what he thinks you are.

Say *oui* [wee] and then what you are in French if he is right. (Remember, *je suis* means "I am"). You are then the next guesser.

Say *non* [naw] if he is wrong and continue until someone is guessed correctly.

Once you have been a guesser, you must think of something else to be (or everyone will know at once what you are).

47

Joke: What must you never do with an enormous mouse? Argue.

Weather

Nobody in the Noisette family can agree about where to go on a rainy day. So Jean has stayed at the chalet with Suzanne and the twins while the others have all set off on different daytrips.

Which of the Noisettes are joking when they phone Suzanne to tell her what the weather is like where they are? Use the word list to find out.

Can you say out loud in French what those who are joking should be saying to Suzanne?

Word list

quel temps fait-il?	what's the weather like?
kel taw faiteel	
il fait beau	it's fine
eel fai bo	
il pleut	it's raining
eel pleuh	
il fait froid	it's cold
eel fai frwa	
il fait chaud	it's hot
eel fai show	
il fait du vent	it's windy
eel fai dew vaw	
il neige	it's snowing
eel nej	
ici	here
eesee	

48

Names

Suzanne	Marie
sewz an	maree

À toi

Quel temps fait-il? [kel taw faiteel]. What's the weather like where you are at the moment? Can you say it in French?

You could write a postcard in French telling someone what the weather is like. Use the word lists, the pictures and the postcard Sophie has written to her friend, Marie, to see how to say all the words you need.

If you are writing to a boy or man you write cher.

This means "How are you?"

Chère Marie,
Comment ça va?
Il fait très chaud ici.
À bientôt,
Sophie.

This means "See you soon". You can write this at the end of a card or letter in French.

Word list

cher/chère..	dear..
shair, shair	
comment ça va?	how are you?
kommaw sa va	
à bientôt	see you soon
ah beea toe	
très	very
trai	

49

Sophie's body game

When everyone returns to the house, the rain is still pouring down. Sophie has made up a game for everyone to play.

Why don't you make Sophie's body game and play it too?

You will need:
a dice,
paper,
pencils or
felt tip pens.

À toi.

le corps

This is the shape you start with.

Word list
à toi — your turn
ah twa
j'ai gagné — I've won
jay ganyay

·	le pied
:·	la main
::	le bras
::	la jambe
::·	la tête
:::	le corps

The idea of the game is to be the first to complete a drawing of a person. Take turns throwing the dice. You must throw a 6 and shout *le corps* [le kor] to start. You can then draw the body.

Use the key above to see which numbers you must throw to add the other parts.

Say the name of each body part in French as you draw it. If you already have the part for the number you throw, pass the dice to the next player. (Remember that you need 2 arms, legs, feet and hands.)

You cannot add hands and feet before the arms and legs.

The first player to complete their person shouts out *la personne* [la pairsonn], and is the winner. *J'ai gagné* [jay ganyay] means "I've won".

Picture list

la personne
la pairsonn
person

la tête
la tet
head

la main
la ma
hand

le bras
le bra
arm

le corps
le kor
body

la jambe
la jomb
leg

le pied
le pee ay
foot

La personne! J'ai gagné.

Making faces

You can play the same game with faces. Cut out lots of eyes, eyebrows, noses, ears and mouths from old magazines. Stick these on paper plates to make up your faces.

You will need:
paper plates, old magazines, scissors, glue and felt tip pens.

Play in the same way as the body game. You must throw a 6 and shout out *les cheveux* [lay sh veuh] to start. Draw on the hair with felt tips.

Check the number on the dice against the key below to see which parts you can then stick on. Remember to say the name of each part in French as you stick it on.

les cheveux

⚀	la bouche
⚁	le nez
⚂	le sourcil
⚃	l'oreille
⚄	l'œil
⚅	les cheveux

La tête! J'ai gagné.

The first one to complete their head with hair, 2 eyes, 2 eyebrows, 2 ears, a nose and a mouth shouts *la tête* [la tet], which means "the head", and is the winner.

Song

Here is a song about faces and bodies to sing in French. Point to each part of the body as you sing about it. You can find the tune on page 64.

La tête, les épaules, les genoux et les orteils,
la tet laze ay paw le lay je noo ay laze or tie
La tête, les épaules, les genoux et les orteils,
la tet laze ay paw le lay je noo ay laze or tie
Les yeux, le nez, la bouche et les oreilles,
laze yeuh le nay la boosh ay laze oh ryee
La tête, les épaules, les genoux et les orteils.
la tet laze ay paw le lay je noo ay laze or tie

Head, shoulders, knees and toes,
Head, shoulders, knees and toes,
Eyes, nose, mouth and ears,
Head, shoulders, knees and toes.

51

Car game

The next day dawns bright and sunny and the Noisettes pile into the car to go to the fair along the coast. It is a long drive so they play a guessing game to pass the time.

The game is to give clues to somewhere and everyone has to guess where this place is.

Il y a [eel ya] means "there is" or "there are". *Du, de la, de l'* and *des* all mean "some".

Madame Noisette starts. She says that at the place she is thinking of *Il y a la mer, du sable, des rochers* [eel ya la mair dew sabl day roshay]. This means "there is the sea, sand, rocks...". Henri guesses *C'est la plage* [sai la plaj] which means "it's the beach". He is right so now it is his turn.

Use the word list to help you see what the others are thinking of. Say the clues out loud, then shout out the right answer from the answer list.

Names

Madame Noisette   Mrs. Noisette
ma dam nwa zet

> ### À toi
> You can play this game too. Just say *il y a* [eel ya] and a few of the words on the word list to describe the place you are thinking about and wait until someone guesses correctly - in French of course.

52

> Il y a des voitures, des rues, des bâtiments...

Word list

il y a eel ya	there is, there are	les fleurs lay flur	flowers
c'est sai	it is	les glaces lay glas	ice cream cones
du, de la, de l', des dew de la de l day	some	les marins lay mara	sailors
le sable le sabl	sand	les arbres laze arbr	trees
la mer la mair	sea	les oiseaux laze wazo	birds
l'argent larjaw	money	les rochers lay roshay	rocks
le comptoir le komtwar	counter	les rues lay rew	streets
les balançoires lay bal onswar	swings	les voitures lay vwa chewr	cars
les bancs lay baw	benches	les bâtiments lay batee maw	buildings
les bateaux lay ba toe	boats	les toboggans lay toe boggaw	slides

Remember that *le* and *la* change to *les* when you are talking about more than one thing (plural). Most words on this list are plurals. You can see the words for one thing (singular) on pages 62 and 63.

> Il y a des balançoires, des toboggans, des bancs...

Answer list

le magasin le magaza	shop, store
la forêt la foray	forest
la plage la plaj	beach
la ville la veel	town
le jardin public le jarda pewbleek	park
le port le por	port

> Il y a des arbres, des fleurs, des oiseaux...

> Qu'est-ce qui
kess kee
est grand et gris et
ai graw ay gree ay
fait "ooooo"?
fai ooo

> Un
an
élé-fantôme.
aylay fontom

53

Joke: What's big and grey and goes "ooooo"? An ele-phantom.

Funny shapes

When they reach the fair, the Noisettes go into the Hall of Mirrors. The mirrors make people look very different from their normal shape and size.

Sophie's reflection is too big. Henri says, *Elle est trop grande* [el ai trow grond], which means "she is too big".

Can you say what is wrong with each person's reflection? Use the word list to find out the words for tall, small, fat and thin.

If it is a boy or a man, say *il est* [eel ai]. If it is a girl or a woman, say *elle est* [el ai].

Elle est trop grande.

Picture list

To describe a boy or man, use the ♂ words.
To describe a girl or woman, use the ♀ words.

♂ petit *ptee*	small	♂ gros *grow*	fat
♀ petite *pteet*		♀ grosse *gross*	
♂ grand *graw*	big, tall	♂ mince *manse*	thin
♀ grande *grond*		♀ mince *manse*	

Word list

| je suis
 je swee | I am | elle est
 el ai | she is |
| trop
 trow | too | il est
 eel ai | he is |

À toi

Are you tall or small? To answer, say *je suis* [je swee] which means "I am" and then the right word (the male ♂ or female ♀ version) from the word list.

Describe your family too, using *il est* (eel ai) for males and *elle est* (el ai) for females.

Joke: What's black and white and very noisy? A penguin playing the trumpet.

55

Hot work

On the way home from the fair, the Noisettes' car breaks down. Setting off on foot, they all realize how hungry or thirsty they are.

Can you see which roads Suzanne and the twins, Delphine, Grand-mère and Monsieur Noisette should take to get what they want?

J'ai faim [jay fa] means "I'm hungry".
J'ai soif [jay swaf] means "I'm thirsty".

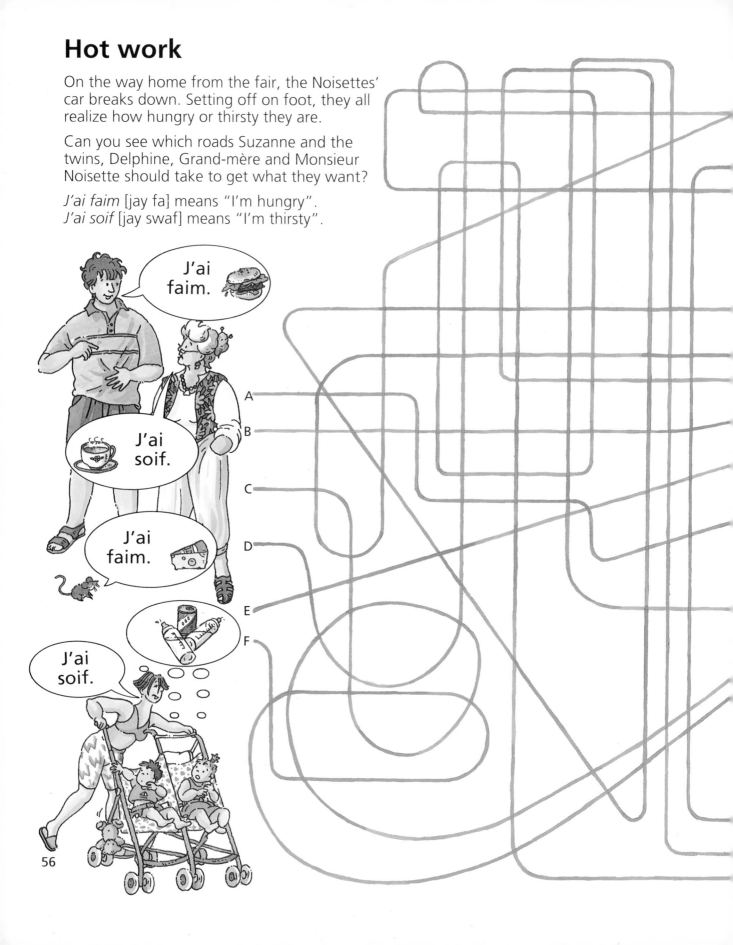

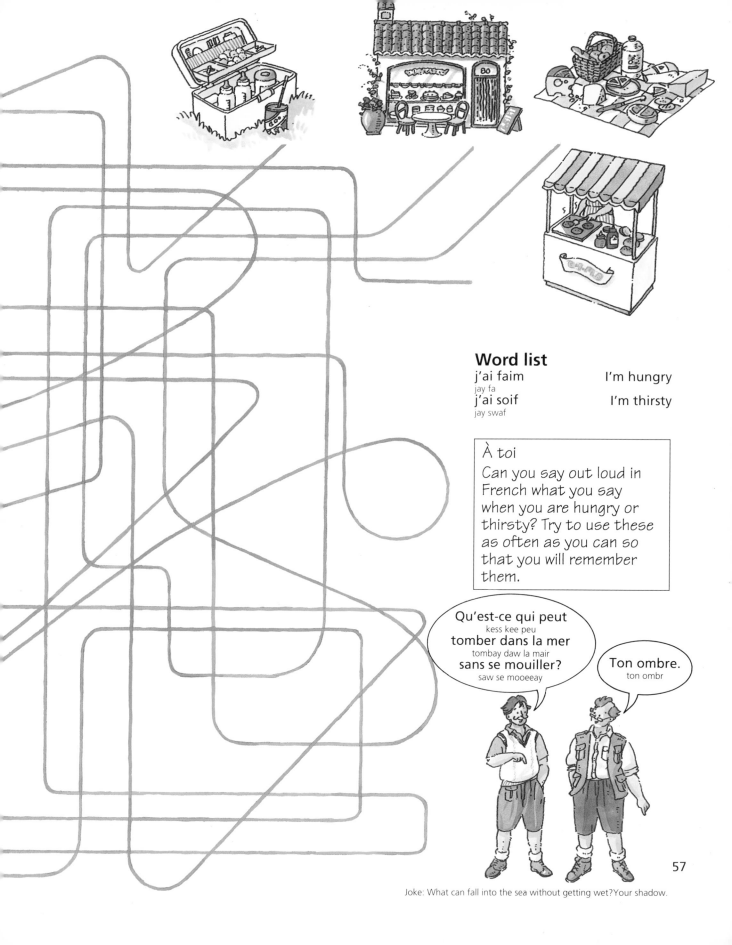

Word list

j'ai faim jay fa	I'm hungry
j'ai soif jay swaf	I'm thirsty

À toi
Can you say out loud in French what you say when you are hungry or thirsty? Try to use these as often as you can so that you will remember them.

Qu'est-ce qui peut
kess kee peu
tomber dans la mer
tombay daw la mair
sans se mouiller?
saw se mooeeay

Ton ombre.
ton ombr

57

Joke: What can fall into the sea without getting wet? Your shadow.

Snapshots

The twins have got hold of some of Henri's photographs and have torn them into pieces. Grand-mère has offered to stick the mixed-up pieces back together. Henri has written a note to help her. Read it to see what Sophie, Oncle Paul and Tante Mirabelle are wearing in the photographs. *Porte* [port] after someone's name means "is wearing" in French. Can you help Grand-mère see which six pieces belong to each photograph?

Quel dommage!

Henri's note

Oncle Paul porte un manteau, une chemise, un pantalon et des chaussures.

Sophie porte un maillot de bain, un chapeau et des bottes.

Tante Mirabelle porte des lunettes de soleil, une jupe, un pull-over et des chaussettes.

58

Use the word list to help you read out loud in French what each person is wearing.

Un [a] and *une* [ewn] both mean "a" as well as "one".

Qu'est-ce qui est
kess kee ai
vert et fait tic-tac?
vair ay fai teek tak

Un concombre
a kon kombr
mécanique.
make an eek

Word list

quel dommage! *kel domaj*	what a pity!
..porte.. *port*	..is wearing..
je porte *je port*	I am wearing
une jupe *ewn jewp*	a skirt
un pull-over *a pewlover*	a pullover
un maillot de bain *a myo de ba*	a swimsuit
un chapeau *a shapo*	a hat
un pantalon *a pontalaw*	trousers
un manteau *a monto*	a coat
une chemise *ewn sh meez*	a shirt
des chaussettes *day show set*	socks

des chaussures *day show sewr*	shoes
des bottes *day bot*	boots
des lunettes de soleil *day lew net de sol eye*	sunglasses
et *ay*	and
qu'est-ce que tu portes? *kess ke tew port*	what are you wearing?

Did you notice that some of the words have *des* [day] before them? This means "some" when you are talking about more than one of that object (plural).

Names

Oncle Paul *onkl pol*	Uncle Paul

À toi

Qu'est-ce que tu portes? [kess ke tew port] What are you wearing? Say *je porte* [je port] and then your clothes. Can you describe what your family or friends are wearing? Here are some more clothes words that you may need.

une robe *ewn rob*	a dress
un tee-shirt *a tee shirt*	a T-shirt
un short *a short*	shorts

59

Joke: What's green and goes tic-toc? A clockwork cucumber.

Going home

It's time for the Noisettes to say goodbye to all the people they have met at the beach.

Au revoir

Au revoir

On the way home, they stop to buy little presents and souvenirs. Jean already knows what he wants to buy - the green flippers.

Can you see what everyone else would like? Use the word list to help you say in French how each person will ask for what he or she wants. Look at the guide opposite to see how to say the describing words on their own.

Je voudrais les palmes vertes s'il vous plaît.

60

Song

Here is a song about a rainbow to sing in French.
You can see what all the words mean on page 64.

Rouge et or-ange et jaune et bleu,
rooj ay or onj ay jone ay bleuh

Vi - o - let, ro - se et vert,
vee o lay ro oze ay vair

Je con-nais les cou - leurs, tou - tes les cou - leurs,
je kon nay lay koo ler too te lay koo ler

De mon arc - en - ciel. Re -
de mon ark aw syell re

-garde a - vec les yeux et chante a - vec la voix,
gard a vek laze yeuh ay shont a vek la vwa

Chante une chan - son gaie.
shont ewn shon saw gay

Je con-nais les cou - leurs, tou - tes les cou - leurs,
je kon nay lay koo ler too te lay koo ler

De mon arc - en - ciel à moi.
de mon ark aw syell ah mwa

À toi
Which object would you most like to have? Can you ask for it in French?

Guide

rouge
rooj

bleu/bleue
bleuh

jaune
jone

rose
roz

vert/verte
vair/vairte

marron
marraw

violet/violette
vee o lay/vee o let

noir/noire
nwar

blanc/ blanche
blaw/blonsh

Some French describing words (called adjectives) change slightly with *la* words. Where there are two words above, use the first one for masculine *le* words and the second one for feminine *la* words. You add a silent "s" if you are describing more than one thing (plural).

61

Word list (part 2)

Here is a list of all the French words and phrases* used in this part of the book in alphabetical order. Use the list either to check quickly what a word means, or to test yourself. The [m] or [f] after l' words tell you whether the word is a le word (masculine) or a la word (feminine).

à bientôt	ah beea toe	*see you soon*
à côté de	ah cotai de	*beside*
à toi	ah twa	*your turn*
arbre (l') [m]	arbr	*tree*
argent (l') [m]	arjaw	*money*
au revoir	orvwar	*goodbye*
balançoire (la)	bal onswar	*swing*
balle (la)	bal	*ball*
banc (le)	baw	*bench*
barrière (la)	ba ree air	*gate*
bateau (le)	ba toe	*boat*
bâtiment (le)	batee maw	*building*
blanc, blanche	blaw, blonsh	*white*
bleu, bleue	bleuh	*blue*
bonjour	bonjoor	*hello*
botte (la)	bot	*boot*
bouche (la)	boosh	*mouth*
bras (le)	bra	*arm*
café (le)	kafay	*café*
camping (le)	kompeeng	*campsite*
canapé (le)	kanapai	*sofa*
canne à pêche (la)	kan a pesh	*fishing rod*
cerf (le)	serr	*deer*
c'est	sai	*it is*
champ (le)	shaw	*field*
chapeau (le)	shapo	*hat*
chat (le)	sha	*cat*
château (le)	sha toe	*castle*
chaumière (la)	show me air	*cottage*
chaussette (la)	show set	*sock*
chaussure (la)	show sewr	*shoe*
chemise (la)	sh meez	*shirt*
cher, chère	shair	*dear*
cheval (le)	shval	*horse*
cheveux (les) [m]	sh veuh	*hair*
chez les Noisette	shay lay nwa zet	*the Noisettes' home*
chien (le)	sheea	*dog*
cinq	sank	*five*
combien (de)	kombeea	*how many*
comment ça va?	kommaw sa va	*how are you?*
comment tu t'appelles?	kommaw tew tapell	*what are you called?*
comptoir (le)	komtwar	*counter*
corbeille à papier (la)	korbaee a papeeay	*wastepaper basket*

corps (le)	kor	*body*
d'accord	dakkor	*OK*
dans	daw	*in*
derrière	derry air	*behind*
deux	deuh	*two*
devant	de vaw	*in front of*
dix	deess	*ten*
du, de la, des	dew, de la, day	*some*
école (l') [f]	aykol	*school*
église (l') [f]	aygleez	*church*
elle	el	*she, it*
elle est	el ai	*she is, it is*
elle porte	el port	*she is wearing*
et	ay	*and*
femme (la)	fam	*woman*
ferme (la)	fairm	*farm*
fille (la)	feey	*girl*
fleur (la)	flur	*flower*
forêt (la)	foray	*forest*
garçon (le)	garssaw	*boy*
gare (la)	gar	*station*
glace (la)	glas	*mirror, ice cream cone*
grand, grande	graw, grond	*big, tall*
grand-mère (la)	gronmair	*grandmother*
gros, grosse	grow, gross	*big, fat*
homme (l') [m]	om	*man*
huit	weet	*eight*
ici	eesee	*here*
il	eel	*he, it*
il est	eel ai	*he is, it is*
il fait beau	eel fai bo	*it's fine*
il fait chaud	eel fai show	*it's hot*
il fait du vent	eel fai dew vaw	*it's windy*
il fait froid	eel fai frwa	*it's cold*
il neige	eel nej	*it's snowing*
il pleut	eel pleuh	*it's raining*
il porte	eel port	*he is wearing*
il y a	eel ya	*there is/there are*
j'ai ...ans	jay aw	*I am...years old*
j'ai faim	jay fa	*I'm hungry*
j'ai gagné	jay ganyay	*I've won*
j'ai soif	jay swaf	*I'm thirsty*
jambe (la)	jomb	*leg*
jardin public (le)	jarda pewbleek	*park*
jaune	jone	*yellow*
je m'appelle	je mapell	*I am called*
je porte	je port	*I am wearing*
je suis	je swee	*I am*
je voudrais	je voodray	*I would like*

62

*Except those in the jokes and songs which are translated on the pages or on the answer page.

French	Pronunciation	English
journal (le)	joornal	newspaper
jupe (la)	jewp	skirt
la voilà	la vwala	there she/it is
lac (le)	lak	lake
lapin (le)	lapa	rabbit
le, la, les	le, la, lay	the
le voilà	le vwala	there he/it is
lit (le)	lee	bed
lunettes de soleil (les) [f]	lew net de sol eye	sunglasses
Madame	ma dam	Mrs.
magasin (le)	magaza	shop, store
maillot de bain (le)	myo de ba	swimsuit
main (la)	ma	hand
maison (la)	mayzaw	house
manteau (le)	monto	coat
marché (le)	marshay	market
marin (le)	mara	sailor
marionnette (la)	mario net	puppet
marron	marraw	brown
mer (la)	mair	sea
merci	mairsee	thank you
mince	manse	thin
moi	mwa	me
Monsieur	missyer	Mr.
moulin à vent (le)	moola a vaw	windmill
mur (le)	mewr	wall
neuf	neuf	nine
nez (le)	nay	nose
nid (le)	nee	nest
noir, noire	nwar	black
non	naw	no
œil (l') [m]	euh ee	eye
oiseau (l') [m]	wazo	bird
oncle (l') [m]	onkl	uncle
orange	oronj	orange
oreille (l') [f]	oh ryee	ear
où est	oo ai	where is
oui	wee	yes
palmes (les) [f]	pal m	flippers
panier (le)	panee ay	basket
panier à linge (le)	panee ay a lanj	laundry basket
pantalon (le)	pontalaw	trousers
papillon (le)	pap ee yaw	butterfly
parapluie (le)	para plewee	umbrella
personne (la)	pairsonn	person
petit, petite	ptee, pteet	small
pied (le)	pee ay	foot
placard (le)	plakar	cupboard
plage (la)	plaj	beach
plante (la)	plont	plant
port (le)	por	harbour
porte-monnaie (le)	port monnai	(money)purse
pull-over (le)	pewlover	pullover
quatre	katr	four
quel âge as-tu?	kel aj a tew	how old are you?
quel dommage!	kel dommaj	what a pity!
quel temps fait-il?	kel taw faiteel	what's the weather like?
qu'est-ce que tu portes?	kess ke tew port	what are you wearing?
radio (la)	radeeo	radio
reine (la)	ren	queen
renard (le)	rnar	fox
rideau (le)	reedo	curtain
robe (la)	rob	dress
rocher (le)	roshay	rock
roi (le)	rwa	king
rose	roz	rose
rouge	rooj	red
rue (la)	rew	street
sable (le)	sabl	sand
sac (le)	sak	bag
salut	salew	hi
seau (le)	so	bucket
sept	set	seven
serpent (le)	sairpaw	snake
serviette (la)	serv ee et	towel
short (le)	short	shorts
s'il vous plaît	seel voo plai	please
six	seess	six
sourcil (le)	soorseel	eyebrow
souris (la)	sooree	mouse
sous	soo	under
sur	sewr	on
table (la)	tabl	table
tambour (le)	tomboor	drum
tante (la)	tont	aunt
tee-shirt (le)	tee shirt	T-shirt
télévision (la)	tay lay veezee aw	television
tente (la)	tont	tent
tête (la)	tet	head
toboggan (le)	toe boggaw	slide
très	trai	very
trois	trwa	three
trop	trow	too
tu es	tew ai	you are
tu portes	tew port	you are wearing
un, une	a, ewn	a, one
vert, verte	vair, vairt	green
ville (la)	veel	town
violet, violette	vee o lay, vee o let	purple
voiture (la)	vwa chewr	car
yeux (les) [m]	yeuh	eyes

Answers (part 2)

PAGE 35
These words have an "x" on the end when there is more than one (plural):

p40-41, p52-53: *l'oiseau* (bird) - *les oiseaux*
p51: *les cheveux* (hair) is already plural
l'œil (eye) - *les yeux*
p52-53: *le bateau* (boat) - *les bateaux*

Here are some more. You can only see the singular (one of them) in this part of the book.

p36-37: *le journal* (newspaper) - *les journaux*
p38-39: *le château* (castle) - *les châteaux*
p44-45: *le rideau* (curtain) - *les rideaux*
le seau (bucket) - *les seaux*
p46-47: *le cheval* (horse) - *les chevaux*
p58-59: *le manteau* (coat) - *les manteaux*
le chapeau (hat) - *les chapeaux*

PAGE 38-39

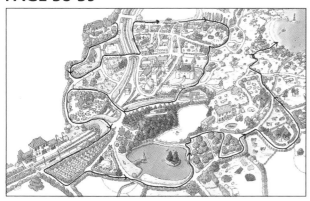

PAGE 40-41
Jean has counted correctly.
Il y a sept arbres. Il y a un nid. Il y a dix fleurs.

PAGE 42-43
Henri is saying *J'ai huit ans.*
Jean is saying *Quel âge as-tu?*
Sophie is saying *J'ai sept ans.*
Either of the twins would say *J'ai un an.*

PAGE 44-45
The box that Jean finds is in the right place:

PAGE 46-47
Claude will say:
Tu es un chien; Tu es un chat; Tu es un garçon;
Tu es une femme; Tu es une reine; Tu es un cheval;
Tu es un oiseau; Tu es un homme.

PAGE 48-49
Grand-mère is joking. She should say *Il fait du vent.*
Madame Noisette is joking. She should say *Il neige.*
Oncle Paul is joking. He should say *Il fait chaud.*

PAGE 50-51

PAGE 52-53
A. *C'est la plage.*   D. *C'est la ville.*
B. *C'est le port.*   E. *C'est le jardin public.*
C. *C'est le magasin.*   F. *C'est la forêt.*

PAGE 56-57
Suzanne and the twins take road F,
Delphine takes road C,
Grand-mère takes road E,
Monsieur Noisette takes road B.

PAGE 58-59
Sophie: Tante Mirabelle: Oncle Paul:
F G I M O R   B D E J L Q   A C H K N P

PAGE 60-61
Francine will say *Je voudrais le porte-monnaie violet*;
Tante Mirabelle will say *Je voudrais le sac bleu*;
Monsieur Noisette will say *Je voudrais les fleurs rouges*;
Madame Noisette will say *Je voudrais les fleurs jaunes*;
Oncle Paul will say *Je voudrais le tambour noir*;
Henri will say *Je voudrais la marionnette marron*;
Sophie will say *Je voudrais la marionnette verte*;
Grand-mère Noisette will say *Je voudrais les bottes blanches.*

Here are the words of the song in English:

Red and orange and yellow and blue,
Purple, pink and green
I know the colours, all the colours,
Of my rainbow.
Look with your eyes and sing with your voice,
Sing a happy song.
I know the colours, all the colours,
Of my very own rainbow.

First French

PART 3: AT SCHOOL

Kathy Gemmell and Jenny Tyler
Illustrated by Sue Stitt
Designed by Diane Thistlethwaite

Consultants: Sarah-Lou Reekie and Kate Griffin

CONTENTS
(part 3)

In this part of the book, the Noisette children are back at school. They are going to help you learn even more French.

Word lists

Don't forget to use the word lists to tell you what the French words mean.

Bonjour
bonjoor

Word list

bonjour	hello
bonjoor	
salut	hi
salew	
moi aussi	me too
mwa oh see	
pardon	sorry
pardaw	
à toi	your turn
ah twa	
où est	where is
le chat?	the cat?
oo ai le sha	
je parle français	I speak French
je parl fronsai	

Salut
salew

Make sure you read the little letters carefully to see how to say each word.

Je parle français.
je parl fronsai

Moi aussi
mwa oh see

Où est le chat?
oo ai le sha

Pardon
pardaw

Remember to try and listen to French people speaking and copy what they say. Here are more clues to help you say some of the sounds which are different from English.

When you see one of these: ç, say it like an "s". Try saying *français* [fronsai] which means "French".

The French "oi" is like the "wa" sound in "wagon". You say the French "au" like the "o" in "rose". Say *moi aussi* [mwa oh see], which means "me too".

The "ch" in French sounds like the "sh" in "show".

Remember to roll French "r"s in the back of your throat and to say the "n"s as if you have a cold.

Try to say out loud what each person on this page is saying.

Can you find Delphine the mouse on every double page in this part of the book?

Games

Here is a game you can play with *le* and *la* words. Count up the number of *le* words (masculine) and *la* words (feminine) on each page.

Say all the *le* words out loud, then shut the book and see how many you can remember. Do the same with the *la* words.

You could play this with a friend. Do it one page at a time. Take turns saying *le* words until one of you can't remember any more. Score a point for each word you can remember after your friend has given up.

Do the same with the *la* words. The winner is the one to score the most points.

À toi
There are à toi boxes in this part of the book as well. Look out for them for extra things to do in French.

Don't forget to look for joke bubbles on some of the pages.

In the classroom

Sophie and Henri Noisette are back at school today. There is a new boy in their class. He introduces himself by saying *Je m'appelle Marc* [je mapell mark]. *Je m'appelle* is how you say "I am called" or "my name is" in French.

Can you help the children introduce themselves to Marc, by saying what's in each speech bubble? Use the word list to help you.

Can you work out which way Marc should go so that he only passes each of them once and ends up at the teacher's desk?

Names

Noisette	**Jean**
nwa zet	jon
Chiffre	**Marc**
sheefr	mark
Roger	**Florence**
ro jay	flor onss
Sophie	**Marie**
sofee	maree
Henri	**Philippe**
onree	fee leep
Francine	**Pierre**
fronseen	pe air

Word list

comment tu t'appelles?	what's your name?
kommaw tew tapell	
je m'appelle	I am called/my name is
je mapell	
il s'appelle	he is called
eel sapell	
elle s'appelle	she is called
el sapell	
ma mère	my mother
ma mair	
mon père	my father
maw pair	
mon frère	my brother
maw frair	
ma sœur	my sister
ma ser	
Monsieur	Mr.
miss yer	
Madame	Mrs.
ma dam	
la grand-mère	grandma
la gronmair	

Je m'appelle Marc.

Je m'appelle Francine.

Je m'appelle Jean.

Je m'appelle Florence.

Je m'appelle Madame Chiffre.

Happy families

Can you match up the people in the column on the right with the person who is talking about them? Use the word list to see what all the words mean.

Je m'appelle Sophie.

Je m'appelle Henri.

Je m'appelle Pierre.

Je m'appelle Philippe.

Je m'appelle Marie.

Ma mère s'appelle Grand-mère Noisette.

Je m'appelle Roger.

Mon père s'appelle Monsieur Noisette.

Je m'appelle Grand-mère Noisette.

Mon frère s'appelle Roger.

Je m'appelle Sophie.

Ma soeur s'appelle Sophie.

Je m'appelle Monsieur Noisette.

What is Henri's sister called?
What is Sophie's father called?
Can you answer in French? *Il s'appelle* [eel sapell] means "he is called" and *elle s'appelle* [el sapell] means "she is called".

À toi
Comment tu t'appelles? [kommaw tew tapell]. What's your name? Try and introduce yourself and your family in French, using the words on this page to help you.

69

How are you?

Look at the picture to see how everyone is this morning.

To ask how someone is in French you say *Comment ça va?* [kommaw sa va] or sometimes just *Ça va?* [sa va] which means, "How are you?"

Madame Chiffre is talking to someone who is saying, "I'm very well, thank you," in French. Use the word list to see how to say this out loud.

Where are they?

Can you spot the following people in the picture?

Someone who has toothache?

Someone with a headache?

Someone who is saying, "My leg hurts"?

Someone with a tummy-ache?

Someone who feels all right?

Use the word list to help you say out loud in French what each person is saying.

Can you spot the words for hand, foot and arm on this page?

le bras
le bra

le pied
le pee ay

At home

Here are some of the Noisette family at home. They should be saying how they feel but the speech bubbles have all been mixed up. Can you say what each person should be saying?

70

Bonjour, ça va?

Ça va très bien, merci.

Ça va?

Ça va?

Ça va bien, merci.

J'ai mal aux dents.

la main
la ma

Word list

bonjour bonjoor	good morning, hello
merci mairsee	thank you
(comment) ça va? kommaw sa va	how are you?
ça va bien sa va bee ai	I'm fine, I'm all right
ça va très bien sa va trai bee ai	I'm very well
j'ai mal aux dents jay mal oh daw	I have toothache
j'ai mal à la tête jay mal ala tet	I have a headache
j'ai mal au ventre jay mal oh vontr	I have a tummy-ache
j'ai mal à la jambe jay mal ala jomb	my leg hurts
la grand-mère la gronmair	grandma
Madame ma dam	Mrs.
Monsieur miss yer	Mr.

Le and *la*

Can you see the words *le* and *la* on this page? Remember that these both mean "the" in French.

In French, all naming words (nouns) are either masculine or feminine. You use *le* for masculine words and *la* for feminine words. Remember to learn words with their *le* or *la*, as you cannot guess which is which.

Before a word starting with a,e,i,o or u, don't forget that you only say the first *l* of *le* or *la*.

J'ai mal à la jambe.

Ça va très bien.

Monsieur Noisette

Roger

À toi

Comment ça va? [kommaw sa va].

How do you feel at the moment? Look at what everyone in the cloakroom is saying to help you say how you feel today. Ask your family and friends how they are in French. You could draw pictures of them and give them French speech bubbles.

Counting

Can you help Sophie with her counting? Look at the first picture to see her counting books. Count the things in the other pictures in the same way, starting with *un* [a], *deux* [deuh].

How many things are in each picture? Answer by saying *il y a* [eel ya] and then the number of things you have counted. Use the word list to see how to say all the words.

Un, deux, trois, quatre, cinq, six, sept, huit, neuf, dix.

Il y a dix livres.

les livres

les plantes

les parapluies

Number list

un a	one	cinq sank	five	huit weet	eight
deux deuh	two	six seess	six	neuf neuf	nine
trois trwa	three	sept set	seven	dix deess	ten
quatre katr	four				

Word list

il y a eel ya	there is, there are	les chapeaux lay shapo	hats
les livres lay leevr	books	les plantes lay plont	plants
les crayons lay krayaw	pencils	les cadeaux lay kado	presents
les parapluies lay para plewee	umbrellas		

Les means "the" when you are talking about more than one object (plural). You don't say *les* after a number.

À toi

Look for things around your house to count. Count them in French. If you want to continue past ten, here are the numbers up to twenty:

onze onz	eleven	seize sez	sixteen
douze dooz	twelve	dix-sept deesset	seventeen
treize trez	thirteen	dix-huit deezweet	eighteen
quatorze katorz	fourteen	dix-neuf deezneuf	nineteen
quinze kanz	fifteen	vingt va	twenty

les cadeaux

Song

Here are the first three verses of a French song. Can you sing it right up to *Dix chats veulent manger...* using all the numbers up to ten in French? Sing it to the tune of "One man went to mow". You can see the tune on page 96 if you don't know it.

Un chat veut manger, veut manger du gâteau,
a sha veuh mawjay veuh mawjay dew ga toe
Un chat et son maître veulent manger du gâteau.
a sha ay saw metr veul maw jay dew ga toe

Deux chats veulent manger, veulent manger
deuh sha veul mawjay veul mawjay
du gâteau,
dew ga toe
Deux chats, un chat et son maître veulent
deuh sha a sha ay saw metr veul
manger du gâteau.
mawjay dew ga toe

Trois chats veulent manger, veulent manger
trwa sha veul mawjay veul mawjay
du gâteau,
dew ga toe
Trois chats, deux chats, un chat et son maître
trwa sha deuh sha a sha ay saw metr
veulent manger du gâteau.
veul mawjay dew ga toe

Here is what it means in English:

One cat wants to eat, wants to eat some cake
One cat and his master want to eat some cake.
Two cats want to eat ...etc.

les crayons

les chapeaux

Qu'est-ce que tu as si
kess ke tew a see
tu croises un éléphant
tew krwaz an ay lay faw
avec un kangourou?
avek a kongaroo

Des
day
trous énormes
troo aynorm
en Australie.
on ostralee

73

Joke: What do you get if you cross an elephant with a kangaroo?
Big holes in Australia.

Days of the week

Sophie and Henri both have timetables to tell them which subject their group will be doing each day.

Using Sophie and Henri's timetables, can you see which day it is in each of the pictures? Say *c'est* [sai] which means "it is" and then the day of the week. Look at the word list to see how to say each of the days.

Word list

c'est sai	it is
lundi lundee	Monday
mardi mardee	Tuesday
mercredi mairkredee	Wednesday
jeudi jeuh dee	Thursday
vendredi vondredee	Friday
samedi samdee	Saturday
dimanche deemonsh	Sunday
le week-end le week end	weekend
le français le fronsai	French
l'anglais longlai	English
le sport le spor	sport
le dessin le dessa	drawing, art
la musique la mewzeek	music

The days of the week do not have capital letters in French.

How many times can you spot the word *le* on these two pages? Remember, *le* is how you say "the" when you are talking about masculine words. For feminine words, "the" is *la*.

Sophie	
lundi	dessin
mardi	français
mercredi	sport
jeudi	anglais
vendredi	musique
samedi	le week-end
dimanche	

Henri	
lundi	sport
mardi	dessin
mercredi	anglais
jeudi	français
vendredi	musique
samedi	le week-end
dimanche	

A

B

A

B

C

D

C

D

Indoor hopscotch

Hopscotch in French is called *la marelle* [la marell]. Here is a type of hopscotch you can play indoors.

Using the word list to help you, write out the days of the week in French on seven squares of paper (each one large enough to put your foot on).

Garçon, il y a
garssaw eel ya
une araignée dans
ewn a renyay daw
ma soupe!
ma soop

Je suis désolé,
je swee day zo lay
monsieur, la mouche
missyer la moosh
est en congé.
et aw konjay

The aim of the game is to collect as many of the paper squares as possible.

Arrange the seven squares on the floor like this with *lundi* (Monday) nearest you:

Stand about 1m (3ft) away from the first square. Throw a coin onto any one of the squares. Say that day out loud in French, using *c'est* and then the day. (If the stone lands between or outside the squares, throw again.)

Then hop up the squares, putting one foot on each of the squares that are side by side, without stepping on the square with the stone on it. You can only hop once on the top square (*dimanche*).

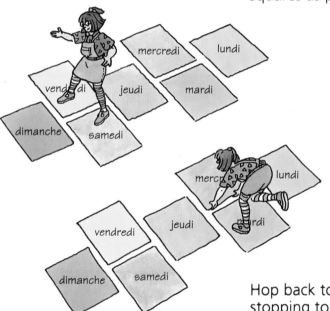

Hop back to the beginning, stopping to pick up the coin and its paper square on the way.

Continue until you have thrown the coin onto all the squares. Remember to say each of the days out loud in French. You will have to hop over wider and wider gaps as you pick up more and more squares.

You can play this game by yourself, or with a friend. If you are playing with a friend, take turns to throw. The winner is the one with the most paper squares at the end.

Joke: Waiter, there's a spider in my soup!
I'm sorry, sir, it's the fly's day off.

À toi
Can you say in French what day it is today? Remember, say *c'est* [sai] then the day.
Try saying what day it is in French every morning for a week.

Putting on a play

Everyone is getting ready for the school play. Most of the children seem to have lost something in the piles of clothes lying around the stage.

To say, "I have lost," in French, say *j'ai perdu* [jay pairdew] and then what you have lost.

Using the word list to help you, can you say in French what each child is saying? *Mon* [maw], *ma* [ma] and *mes* [may] all mean "my".

Can you find all the lost objects? Point to each one and say, "there it is" or "there they are". This is *le voilà* [le vwala] for *le* words (the ones with *mon* before them), *la voilà* [la vwala] for *la* words (the ones with *ma* before them) or *les voilà* [lay vwala] for the words with *mes* before them (plural).

76

Word list

j'ai perdu [jay pairdew]	I have lost	mon crayon [maw krayaw]	my pencil
mes gants [may gaw]	my gloves	ma trousse [ma trooss]	my pencil case
ma ceinture [ma santewr]	my belt	mes feutres [may feutr]	my felt tips
ma montre [ma montr]	my watch	mon cahier [maw kaeeay]	my exercise book
mon gilet [maw jeelay]	my cardigan	et [ay]	and
mes lunettes [may lewnet]	my glasses	le/la voilà [le/la vwala]	there it is
mon chapeau [maw shapo]	my hat	les voilà [lay vwala]	there they are

À toi

Here is a French memory game that you can play with two or more players. One person starts by saying *j'ai perdu* [jay pairdew] and then the name of an object in French. You can use any of the objects on this page.

Take turns repeating what the person before has said and then adding another object to the list. To say "and" in French, you say *et* [ay]. You are out if you can't remember everything in the right order or can't think of an object to add. The winner is the last one to be out.

Art class

Francine has painted a picture of an animal she particularly likes, using her favourite colour.

Look how she says which colour and animal she likes best.

Can you see which is Francine's painting?

Use the word list to help you match each of Francine's friends with their pictures.

Word list

mon animal préféré est..	my favourite animal is..
mon anee mal prai fai rai ai	
ma couleur préférée est le/l'..	my favourite colour is..
ma kooler prai fai rai ai le	
le chat	the cat
le sha	
le chien	the dog
le sheea	
le lapin	the rabbit
le lapa	
la souris	the mouse
la sooree	
le cheval	the horse
le shval	
l'éléphant	the elephant
laylayfaw	
le cochon	the pig
le ko shaw	

One animal on the word list isn't anyone's favourite. Can you spot which one it is?

À toi
Tell someone in French what colour you like best. Try saying what your favourite animal is. You can use what Francine's friends are saying to help you.

Ma couleur préférée est l'orange. Mon animal préféré est le cheval.

Ma couleur préférée est le jaune. Mon animal préféré est le lapin.

Ma couleur préférée est le marron. Mon animal préféré est la souris.

Pourquoi les
poorkwa laze
éléphants sont-ils
aylayfaw sonteel
grands et gris?
graw ay gree

Parce que s'ils
parss ke seelz
étaient petits et blancs,
aitai ptee ay blaw
ils seraient des flocons
eel serai day flokaw
de neige.
de nej

Ma couleur
préférée est le vert.
Mon animal préféré
est le chat.

Ma couleur
préférée est le rouge.
Mon animal préféré
est le chien.

Ma couleur
préférée est le bleu.
Mon animal préféré
est le cochon.

Colour guide

bleu (bleue)
bleuh
rouge
rooj
vert (verte)
vair, vairt
orange
oronj
jaune
jone
violet (violette)
vee o lay, vee o let
blanc (blanche)
blaw, blonsh
noir (noire)
nwar
marron
marraw

French colour words often
change slightly when they
are used to describe particular
objects. You use the first word
above to describe masculine *le*
things. The words in brackets
describe feminine *la* things.
On this page, you use the first
word on the guide.

79

Joke: Why are elephants big and grey?
Because if they were small and white they'd be snowflakes.

French calendar

Sophie and her friends are making French calendars which last for twelve years. You can make one too by following the instructions below.

You will need:
2 sheets of cardboard about 29cm by 21cm (11in by 8in), scissors, pencils and felt tip pens, a ruler and some glue.

Use the word list to find out the names of the months in French. Look back at page 74 if you can't remember which day of the week is which.

1. Use the ruler to draw 3cm (1in) squares over one of the sheets of cardboard, then cut the sheet into strips lengthwise (each strip 3cm (1in) wide).

2. Each strip will have just over nine squares on it. On the first strip, leave one full blank square at either end, then write in the days of the week in French, one on each square, like this:

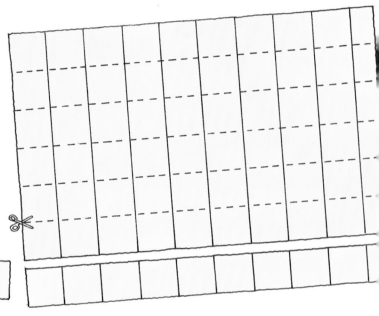

| | lundi | mardi | mercredi | jeudi | vendredi | samedi | dimanche | | | |

3. Stick the next two strips together to make one very long strip and mark numbers 1-16 on one side, again leaving a blank square at either end. Don't cut these off. Draw 3cm (1in) squares on the other side and write in numbers 17-31.

| | 1 | 2 | 3 | 4 | 5 | 6 | 7 | 8 | 9 | 10 | 11 | 12 | 13 | 14 | 15 | 16 | |

| | 17 | 18 | 19 | 20 | 21 | 22 | 23 | 24 | 25 | 26 | 27 | 28 | 29 | 30 | 31 | |

Word list

janvier	January	juillet	July	l'hiver	winter
jonveeay		*jooeeay*		*leevair*	
février	February	août	August	le printemps	spring
fave reeay		*oot*		*le prantaw*	
mars	March	septembre	September	l'été	summer
marss		*septombr*		*laitai*	
avril	April	octobre	October	l'automne	autumm
avreel		*octobr*		*lo tonn*	
mai	May	novembre	November		
may		*novombr*			
juin	June	décembre	December		
jwah		*daysombr*			

French people don't spell months, seasons, nor days of the week with capital letters.

4. On the next strip write the months in French: *janvier* to *juin* on one side and *juillet* to *décembre* on the other. This time you will have more than one square left over. Don't cut them off as you will need them to pull the strips through the calendar.

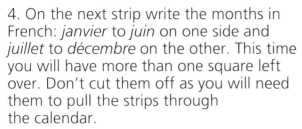

5. The last strip is for the years. Write 1993 to 1998 on one side and 1999 to 2004 on the other.

6. Mark off the second sheet as shown below:

Cut slots along the lines. Thread your strips through to show the right day, date, month and year.

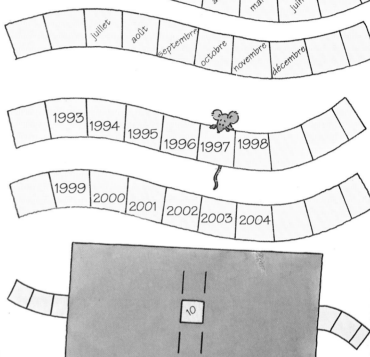

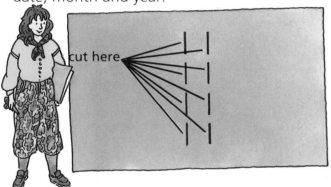

Sophie and the others are decorating an enormous calendar they have made for the classroom.

You could decorate the front of your calendar too, using the different seasons.

Comment
kommaw
s'appelle un bébé qui
sappela baibai kee
est né en mars?
ai nayaw marss

Un martien
a marsseea

Joke: What do you call a baby born in March? A martian.

What is it?

Madame Chiffre has divided the class into teams to play a guessing game. The teams wear blindfolds and take turns to pick objects out of a large box. They must guess what they have picked out.

To ask what something is in French, you say *est-ce que c'est...?* [ess ke sai], which means "is it...?" and then the name of the object.

To answer, you say *oui, c'est...* [wee sai], which means "yes, it's...", or *non, ce n'est pas...* [naw, se nai pa], which means "no, it's not...".

Using the word list to help you, can you answer everyone's questions?

Can you now tell the people who have guessed wrongly what their objects are, using *c'est* [sai] and then the name of the object? So you would say to Sophie, *C'est un coquillage* [sait a kokeeaj].

Word list

est-ce que c'est...? *ess ke sai*	is it...?	une sucette *ewn sewset*	a lollipop
oui *wee*	yes	un cerf-volant *a sair volaw*	a kite
non *naw*	no	un coquillage *a kokeeaj*	a shell
c'est *sai*	it is	un livre *a leevr*	a book
ce n'est pas *se nai pa*	it is not	une montre *ewn montr*	a watch
un pipeau *a peepo*	a recorder	un porte-monnaie *a port monay*	a purse
un sifflet *a seeflay*	a whistle	un crayon *a krayaw*	a pencil
une raquette *ewn rackett*	a racket		

Est-ce que c'est une sucette?

Oui, c'est une sucette.

Est-ce que c'est un porte-monnaie?

Est-ce que c'est un livre?

Est-ce que c'est un pipeau?

Non, ce n'est pas un pipeau.

Est-ce que c'est un pipeau?

Song

Here is a song to sing in French. Can you guess what any of the words mean? You can check what they all mean on page 96.

Qu'est-ce que c'est que je vois là? Est-ce que c'est un gros vieux rat?
kess ke sai ke je vwa la ess ke sait a grow veeyeuh ra

Ce n'est pas un poiss - on rouge, ni un é - lé - phant qui bouge,
Se nai paz a pwass aw rooj nee an ay lay faw kee booj

Qu'est-ce que c'est que je vois là? Ça va, c'est mon pe - tit chat.
kess ke sai ke je vwa la sa va sai maw peuh tee sha

Est-ce que c'est un cerf-volant?

Est-ce que c'est un coquillage?

Qu'est-ce qui a huit
kess kee a weet
jambes, deux roues
jomb deuh roo
et qui va très vite?
ay kee va trai veet

Une araignée
ewn a renyay
à moto.
a moto

Est-ce que c'est un cerf-volant?

Est-ce que c'est un sifflet?

83

Joke: What has eight legs, two wheels and goes very fast?
A spider on a motorbike.

Hide and seek

During break, Francine and Henri are playing hide and seek. It's Henri's turn to hide. Can you spot him? (If you can't remember who Henri is, look back to page 69.)

To say, "There he is," in French, you say *Le voilà* [le vwala].

Où est Francine? [oo ai fronseen]. Where is Francine? To say, "There she is", you say *La voilà* [la vwala].

Can you find which paths Francine must take to reach Henri by the shortest route? She cannot use any of the paths which are blocked by children or objects.

Word list

où est oo ai	where is
le voilà le vwala	there he,it is
la voilà la vwala	there she,it is
le drapeau le dra po	flag
le chat le sha	cat
la souris la sooree	mouse
le vélo le vaylo	bicycle
le cerf-volant le sair volaw	kite
le jardinier le jardeeneeay	gardener

Can you spot some other things in the picture? Say *Le voilà* [le vwala] when you spot a *le* object and *La voilà* when you find a *la* object.

Où est le cerf-volant?

Où est le chat?

Où est le vélo?

Où est le drapeau?

84 Où est la souris?

Joke: What goes thththththth?
A snake with a lisp.

Tongue twister

How fast can you say this tongue twister without making any mistakes?

Un chasseur sachant
a shasser sashaw
chasser doit savoir chasser
shassay dwah savvar shassay
sans son chien.
saw saw sheea

85

Here is what it means in English: A hunter who knows how to hunt should know how to hunt without his dog.

Sports day

Today is sports day. Madame Chiffre is asking who knows how to climb, *Qui sait grimper?* [kee sai grampay]. Sophie answers, *Je sais grimper* [je sais grampay] which means, "I know how to climb".

Use the word list opposite to help you answer these questions for the people in the picture. Point to someone who is doing each activity and say *je sais* [je sai] for them and then what he or she is doing.

Qui sait faire le poirier?
Qui sait courir?
Qui sait ramper?
Qui sait faire des cabrioles?
Qui sait faire la roue?
Qui sait marcher à cloche-pied?
Qui sait sauter?

À toi
Do you know how to do any of the things in the picture? Look at the word list to see how to say what you can do in French. Remember, say *je sais* [je sai] and then what you can do.

Joke: Doctor, the invisible man's waiting for you. Tell him that I can't see him.

Word list

qui sait...? kee sai	who can/knows how...?	**faire des galipettes** fair day galeepet	to do somersaults
je sais je sai	I can/know how	**marcher à cloche-pied** marshay a klosh pee ay	to hop
sais-tu...? sai tew	can you...?	**ramper** rompay	to crawl
courir kooreer	to run	**grimper** grampay	to climb
faire le poirier fair le pwareeay	to do a handstand	**sauter** so tay	to jump
faire la roue fair la roo	to do a cartwheel		

French flip-flaps

Here is how to make and use a French flip-flap.

You will need:

a large square of paper and some felt tips.

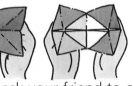

Fold each corner of your paper square into the middle. Turn the paper over and do the same on the other side.

Write numbers 2 to 9, one on each of the small triangles you can now see.

Lift up the four flaps in turn. Under each number, write down *sais-tu* [sai tew], which means "can you" followed by one of the activites from the word list. You will have to write in little writing to fit in all the words.

Fold the flaps in again and turn the square back over.

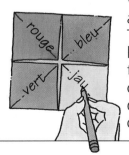

Write *bleu, rouge, jaune* and *vert* on the four small squares. Fill them in with your felt tips. (Look back at page 78 if you can't remember which ones to use).

Slide both your index fingers and thumbs under the squares and push them together like this:

Ask a friend to choose a square. Say the word on it, then do this as you spell it out:

Now ask your friend to choose a number. Count it out in French, opening your flip-flap to the top and side as before. (If you can't remember all the numbers in French, look back at page 72.)

When you finish counting, ask your friend to choose another number. This time, open up that flap and read out loud in French what it says under the number your friend has chosen. Your friend must do the activity you read, or start again.

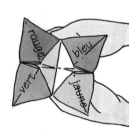

Lunchtime

Today, lunch is outside. Unfortunately, not everyone seems to be having a good time.

Cathy [katee] is in a bad mood because she has ripped her skirt. *Je suis de mauvaise humeur* [je swee de mo vaze ewmur] means, "I am in a bad mood," in French.

How do you think the other children are feeling? Use the word list to help you match each speech bubble below with a child in the picture. Can you say each one out loud in French?

J'ai soif.

J'ai faim.

J'ai chaud.

J'ai froid.

J'ai soif.

J'ai faim.

Je suis content.

Je suis fatigué.

J'ai faim.

Je suis triste.

À toi

How *do* you feel at the moment?

Use the word list to describe how you feel in French. Remember to use the extra "e" on the end of the words for happy and tired if you are a girl.

Je suis de mauvaise humeur.

Donne-moi les noms de
don mwa lay naw de
trente animaux qui
tront anee mo kee
viennent d'Afrique.
vee en dafreek

Vingt-neuf
vant neuf
éléphants et une
ay lay faw ay ewn
girafe.
jee raf

88

Joke: Give me the names of 30 animals which come from Africa.
29 elephants and a giraffe.

Word list

In French, some describing words (adjectives) are slightly different for boys and girls. Where there are two words together on this list, use the first to describe a boy and the second to describe a girl.

j'ai faim jay fa		I'm hungry
j'ai soif jay swaf		I'm thirsty
j'ai chaud jay show		I'm hot
j'ai froid jay frwa		I'm cold
je suis je swee		I am

content, contente kontaw, kontont	happy
triste treest	sad
fatigué, fatiguée fateegay, fateegay	tired
de mauvaise humeur de mo vaze ewmur	in a bad mood

Telling the time

Suzanne must meet Sophie and Francine from school today but her watch is broken so she has to keep asking the time.

To ask the time in French, you say *Quelle heure est-il?* [keller aiteel]. To answer, you say *il est* [eel ai] which means "it is" and then the time.

Heures [ur] after a number on the clock means "o'clock".

So to say, "It's 10 o'clock," in French, you say *Il est dix heures* [eel ai deezer]. How do you say, "It's six o'clock"?

Can you say *Il est ... heures* for each of the hours on Grand-mère Noisette's alarm clock?

Now can you spot what time it is in each of these pictures? Answer Suzanne's question in each one by saying the time out loud in French. Use Grand-mère Noisette's alarm clock to help you with the numbers.

Word list

quelle heure est-il? keller aiteel	what time is it?
il est...heures eel ai..ur	it's...o'clock
...et demie ay demee	half past...
midi meedee	midday
minuit meenwee	midnight

You don't say *heures* after *midi* or *minuit*.

midi / minuit
meedee meenwee

onze heures
onzer

dix heures
deezer

neuf heures
neuffer

huit heures
weeter

sept heures
setter

six heures
seezer

une heure
ewn ur

deux heures
deuzer

trois heures
trwazer

quatre heures
katrer

cinq heures
sanker

Il est huit heures.

Quelle heure est-il?

A

B

C

D

E

À toi

Quelle heure est-il? [keller aiteel]. Can you say in French what time it is at the moment? Say it to the nearest half hour. If you want to say "half-past" you say *et demie* [ay demee] after the hour. To say "half-past four" you would say *quatre heures et demie* [katrer ay demee].

91

True or false?

Francine and Sophie are playing a game on the way home from school. One of them says something and the other has to say whether it is true or false.

To say, "It's true," in French, you say *C'est vrai* [sai vrai]. To say, "It's false," you say *C'est faux* [sai fo].

Can you say what the reply to each of their speech bubbles should be? Say the answers out loud. If you don't know, say *Je ne sais pas* [je ne sai pa] which means, "I don't know".

Look back through the book if you can't remember any of the words.

Word list

c'est vrai	it's true
sai vrai	
c'est faux	it's false
sai fo	
je ne sais pas	I don't know
je ne sai pa	
voici	here is
vwasee	

Il y a trois cerfs-volants.

Mon livre est bleu.

Mon frère s'appelle Grand-mère Noisette.

What's the right word?

Madame Chiffre stays late at school to correct everyone's work. Can you help her? Say out loud in French what should be written under each picture.

Voici [vwasee] means "here is". Look back through this part of the book if you can't remember any of the words you need.

Voici un cochon.

Voici un parapluie.

Voici un coquillage.

Voici ma mère.

Voici une montre.

À toi

You could make your own word and picture book in French. Draw something then write what it is in French, using *voici* [vwasee] and then the name of the object. Remember to check if it is a *le* or a *la* object, so that you know whether to write *un* (for *le* words) or *une* (for *la* words) before it.

Word list (part 3)

Here is a list of all the French words and phrases* used in this part of the book in alphabetical order. Use the list either to check quickly what a word means, or to test yourself.

Cover up the English words and see if you can remember what each French word means. Do the same the other way around, covering up the French and saying the French for each English word.

The [m] or [f] after *l'* or *les* words tell you whether the word is a *le* word (masculine) or a *la* word (feminine).

à toi	ah twa	your turn
anglais (l') [m]	onglai	English
animal (l') [m]	anee mal	animal
août	oot	August
automne (l') [m]	oh tonn	autumn
avril	avreel	April
blanc, blanche	blaw, blonsh	white
bleu, bleue	bleuh	blue
bonjour	bonjoor	hello
bras (le)	bra	arm
ça va bien	sa va beeai	I'm fine
ça va très bien	sa va trai beeai	I'm very well
cadeau (le)	kado	present
cahier (le)	kaeeay	exercise book
ce n'est pas	se nai pa	it is not
ceinture (la)	santewr	belt
cerf-volant (le)	sair volaw	kite
c'est	sai	it is, that is
c'est faux	sai fo	that's false
c'est vrai	sai vrai	that's true
chapeau (le)	shapo	hat
chat (le)	sha	cat
cheval (le)	shval	horse
chien (le)	sheea	dog
cinq	sank	five
cochon (le)	ko shaw	pig
comment ça va?	kommaw sa va	how are you?
comment tu t'appelles?	kommaw tew tapell	what's your name?
content, contente	kontaw, kontont	happy
coquillage (le)	kokeeaj	shell
couleur (la)	kooler	colour
courir	kooreer	to run
crayon (le)	krayaw	pencil

de mauvaise humeur	de mo vaze ewmur	in a bad mood
décembre	daysombr	December
dessin (le)	dessa	drawing, art
deux	deuh	two
dimanche (le)	deemonsh	Sunday
dix	deess	ten
dix-huit	deezweet	eighteen
dix-neuf	deezneuf	nineteen
dix-sept	deesset	seventeen
douze	dooz	twelve
drapeau (le)	dra po	flag
école (l') [f]	aykol	school
éléphant (l') [m]	aylayfaw	elephant
elle s'appelle	el sapell	she is called
est-ce quec'est...?	ess ke sai	is it...?
et	ay	and
...et demie	ay demee	half past...
été (l') [m]	ai tai	summer
faire des cabrioles	fair day kabreeole	to do somersaults
faire la roue	fair la roo	to do a cartwheel
faire le poirier	fair le pwareeay	to do a handstand
fatigué, fatiguée	fateegay	tired
feutre (le)	feutr	felt tip pen
février	fave reeay	February
français (le)	fronsai	French
frère (le)	frair	brother
gants (les) [m]	gaw	gloves
gilet (le)	jeelay	cardigan
grand-mère (la)	gronmair	grandma
grimper	grampay	climb
hiver (l') [m]	eevair	winter
huit	weet	eight
il est ... heures	eel ai ... ur	its ... o'clock
il s'appelle	eel sapell	he is called
il y a	eel ya	there is, there are
j'ai chaud	jay show	I'm hot
j'ai faim	jay fa	I'm hungry
j'ai froid	jay frwa	I'm cold
j'ai mal à la jambe	jay mal ala jomb	my leg hurts
j'ai mal à la tête	jay mal ala tet	I have a headache
j'ai mal au ventre	jay mal oh vontr	I have a tummy-ache
j'ai mal aux dents	jay mal oh daw	I have toothache
j'ai perdu	jay pairdew	I have lost
j'ai soif	jay swaf	I'm thirsty
janvier	jonveeay	January

94

*Except those in the jokes and songs which are translated on the pages or on the answer page.

French	Pronunciation	English
jardinier (le)	jardeeneeay	gardener
jaune	jone	yellow
je m'appelle	je mapell	I am called
je ne sais pas	je ne sai pa	I don't know
je parle français	je parl fronsai	I speak French
je sais	je sai	I know (how to)
je suis	je swee	I am
jeudi (le)	jeuh dee	Thursday
juillet	jooeeay	July
juin	jwah	June
la voilà	la vwala	there she, it is
lapin (le)	lapa	rabbit
le, la, les	le, la, lay	the
le voilà	le voilà	there he, it is
les voilà	lay vwala	there they are
livre (le)	leevr	book
lundi (le)	lundee	Monday
lunettes (les) [f]	lewnet	glasses
Madame	ma dam	Mrs.
mai	may	May
main (la)	ma	hand
marcher à cloche-pied	marshay a klosh pee ay	to hop
mardi (le)	mardee	Tuesday
marelle (la)	la marell	hopscotch
marron	marraw	brown
mars	marss	March
merci	mairsee	thank you
mercredi (le)	mairkredee	Wednesday
mère (la)	mair	mother
midi	meedee	midday
minuit	meenwee	midnight
moi aussi	mwa oh see	me too
mon, ma, mes	maw, ma, may	my
Monsieur	miss yer	Mr.
montre (la)	montr	watch
musique (la)	mewzeek	music
neuf	neuf	nine
noir, noire	nwar	black
non	naw	no
novembre	novombr	November
octobre	octobr	October
oncle (l') [m]	onkl	uncle
onze	onz	eleven
orange	oronj	orange
où est	oo ai	where is
oui	wee	yes
parapluie (le)	para plewee	umbrella
pardon	pardaw	sorry
père (le)	pair	father
pied (le)	pee ay	foot
pipeau (le)	peepo	recorder
plante (la)	plont	plant
portemonnaie (le)	port monnai	purse
préféré, préférée	prai fai rai	favourite
printemps (le)	prantaw	spring
quatorze	katorz	fourteen
quatre	katr	four
quelle heure est-il?	keller aiteel	what time is it?
qui sait...?	kee sai	who knows (how to)...?
quinze	kanz	fifteen
ramper	rompay	to crawl
raquette (la)	rackett	racket
rouge	rooj	red
sais-tu...?	sai tew	do you know (how to)...?
salut	salew	hi
samedi (le)	samdee	Saturday
sauter	so tay	to jump
seize	sez	sixteen
sept	set	seven
septembre	septombr	September
sifflet (le)	seeflay	whistle
six	seess	six
sœur (la)	ser	sister
souris (la)	sooree	mouse
sport (le)	spor	sport
sucette (la)	sewset	lollipop
tante (la)	tont	aunt
treize	trez	thirteen
triste	treest	sad
trois	trwa	three
trousse (la)	trooss	pencil case
un, une	a, ewn	a, one
vélo (le)	vaylo	bicycle
vendredi (le)	vondredee	Friday
vert, verte	vair, vairt	green
vingt	va	twenty
violet, violette	vee o lay, vee o let	purple
voici	vwasee	here is
week-end (le)	weekend	week-end

Answers (part 3)

PAGE 68-69
This is the way Marc should go:

Here are the French answers to the questions:
Elle s'appelle Sophie.
Il s'appelle Monsieur Noisette.

PAGE 70-71
Madame Noisette should say, *J'ai mal à la jambe.*
Grand-mère Noisette should say, *Ça va très bien.*
Monsieur Noisette should say, *J'ai mal à la tête.*
Roger should say, *J'ai mal au ventre.*

PAGE 72-73
Il y a huit plantes.   *Il y a neuf crayons.*
Il y a trois parapluies.   *Il y a sept chapeaux.*
Il y a cinq cadeaux.

Here is the tune for the song:

1. Un chat veut man - ger, veut man-ger du gâ - teau,
a sha veuh maw jay veuh maw jay dew ga toe

Un chat et son maître veulent man-ger du gâ - teau.
a sha ay saw metr veul maw jay dew ga toe

2. Deux chats veulent man - ger, veulent man-ger du gâ - teau
deuh sha veul maw jay veul maw jay dew ga toe

Deux chats, un chat et son maître veulent man-ger du gâ - teau.
deuh sha a sha ay saw metr veul maw jay dew ga toe

3. Trois chats veulent man - ger, veulent man-ger du gâ - teau,
trwa sha veul maw jay veul maw jay dew ga toe

Trois chats, deux chats, un chat et son maître veulent man-ger du gâ-teau.
trwa sha deuh sha a sha ay saw metr veul maw jay dew ga toe

PAGE 74-75
A. *C'est lundi.*   C. *C'est vendredi.*
B. *C'est jeudi.*   D. *C'est mardi.*

PAGE 78-79

L'éléphant (the elephant) isn't anyone's favourite.

PAGE 82-83
This is what the words mean in English:
What is it that I see there?
Is it a big old rat?
It's not a goldfish,
Nor an elephant moving,
What is it that I see there?
It's OK, it's my little cat.

PAGE 84-85
This is the way Francine should go:

PAGE 90-91
A. *Il est neuf heures.*   D. *Il est trois heures.*
B. *Il est onze heures.*   E. *Il est quatre heures.*
C. *Il est une heure.*

PAGE 92-93
A. *C'est faux.*   C. *C'est faux.*   E. *C'est faux.*
B. *C'est vrai.*   D. *C'est vrai.*   F. *C'est faux.*

Here is what should be written under each picture:
A. *Voici un chien.*   D. *Voici un crayon*
B. *Voici un livre.*   E. *Voici mon père.*
C. *Voici un chapeau.*